New World Order: The Mad Tyrant

Craig Claridge

Copyright © 2018 Craig Claridge

All rights reserved.

ISBN: 9781718066670

DEDICATION

I would like to dedicate this book to anybody who has ever believed in me. But mainly to my two special girls. My wife Stacey Claridge and my daughter who is due three weeks from this book being published. I love you both to the moon and back.

CONTENTS

	Prologue	1
1	My Life	3
2	Pack Attack	14
3	Ray Miller	24
4	The Pursuit	34
5	Wanted: Dead or Alive	48
6	A New Hybrid	60
7	Faith Fear	68
8	The Faceless Leader	77
9	The Masquerade Ball	88
10	The Assassination	104
11	The Attack	115
12	The Infiltration	128
13	The Rescue	141
14	Reunion	159
15	The Future	172

Prologue

Wasteland. All around me. What once used to be a bustling city of activity, reduced to nothing. Rubble. The city that never sleeps turned to the city that always sleeps. A city of 8 million people reduced to a few hundred and deteriorating all the time. Of course the same could be said about the entire planet. The year is 2048. At a time when we thought the world would be advanced with flying cars and robots, it's at its worst.

It happened thirty years ago. Tensions were building between all countries. There were wars in the middle east, in Asia and Africa. Russia and USA with all their nuclear arsenal were at each others throats. Everyone knew it was only a matter of time. And then the missiles started firing. Within seconds, what was once green and alive turned grey and dead. Smog covered the planet and blotted out the sun. Everything turned colder. There were some that saw it coming and hid deep underground in nuclear bunkers built for such a thing. Others weren't so fortunate.

As the smog covered the Earth and became uninhabitable, the deaths began. The blasts themselves wiped out 3 billion. Most turned to nothing but ashes and dust and then the rest caught in the blast radius. Then every year another billion would die from the contamination and lack of food. The whole world suddenly delved into a state of poverty. There was only limited amounts of food and water savoured from before.

By 2022 the worlds population was reduced to below one million. The whole planet, what was left of it, decided enough was enough. It was time to come out from underground. As the world emerged coughing, something happened. Humans had evolved. During the time underground it was clear at least some of the contamination had made its way underground. And now as everyone came out into the open, everybody could breathe. Survival of the fittest still true even in its darkest days. And what's my story in this.

I'm just coming to that

Chapter 1

My Life

I was born Blake Andrews, in the year of 2024. I'd heard all the stories of what the world was like from my dad. The breeze of fresh air flowing through your hair as spring approached. The hot sun beaming down on your skin in the summer. The crunch of leaves underfoot that had fallen from trees in Autumn. And the chill of the icy wind in the winter.

I had never felt any of this. I can only imagine what it may have felt like. Now there are no seasons. Every day a dreary one with dust settling all around. Buildings demolished and run into the ground. Old vehicles burned and destroyed. Plant life, there is no plant life. If it wasn't for evolution, humans would be extinct.

My mother died during childbirth. With there being no doctors around mixed with the strain of the contamination, it was too much for her to handle. My father loved my mother. I could tell by the way he used to describe her. She had long, golden blonde hair down to her shoulders and dark blue eyes. She had a slim figure before she was pregnant and my dad always said she always smelled like she was constantly wearing perfume. Even after the end of the world, she still smelled like fresh flowers. And so it was up to my dad to raise me. To protect me. And maybe most importantly, give me a picture of what the world used to look like. My dad was once a general in what was the U.S army. He knew before a lot of people that war was imminent. It was mainly for this reason he and my mum survived. He had been preparing for a couple of years storing the many items needed to survive underground. Then when it started he risked court-martial but he knew it wouldn't happen because he knew that this would be the end. And so he took my mother and himself underground to hopefully survive first the blast and second the contamination.

But even all that preparation wouldn't be enough. Rationing was hard and the supplies wasn't going to last forever. So it was time to emerge with what little they had left in 2022. He always said that the first five seconds that they emerged was the hardest in his life. There was no air. He thought he would die there and then with my mother. It seemed to last a lifetime. But then incredibly air reached his lungs. He could breathe. He knew humans had evolved. Charles Darwin's theory just proved to be even more true.

And so he began to look around. He began to search for something. Anything. But nothing was to be found. He couldn't even be sure if they were the only ones to have survived. But he thought surely there were others that foresaw it. All the many priests around the world with their different Gods. The people that society used to call crazy ranting about the end of the world. It seems that society was crazy for not listening. But there was no one. All he could hear was the rustle of wind. The dust kicking up and stinging their eyes. They were about to travel to look for food or shelter when they saw something.

In the distance, they could see a pack of what looked like wolves surrounding a carcass. From where they stood they couldn't tell what the carcass was but they didn't care. They were just happy to see that some creatures had survived. At least they thought they'd be happy. That was until one of the wolves turned around. It was clear that these weren't the wolves once of Earth but something different entirely.

They were a type of wolves hybrid. There was still a bit of wolf left. But these were monstrous. The teeth had grown into a grotesque set of fangs. They had a mixture of blood and saliva oozing from the mouth. Huge chunks of fur had been ripped out. They looked like demon dogs. And one of them had their bloodcurdling eyes on my dad. I remember him saying that he thought that would be the end of him and my mother. But luckily my dad was always quick witted and managed to duck behind a huge boulder that was near him. My mother and father just stayed there for about 5 minutes watching the wolves tearing apart the carcass. They eventually finished and went the other way. But it was clear that it wouldn't be the last of them and it begged the question. Were there other hybrids out there? To this day I still don't know. I've stayed in New York all my life living off the contaminated land and I still haven't seen another hybrid other than the wolf.

A couple of years passed with my parents learning to adapt and survive in this new, poisoned world. And they found out they were to have their first child. Of course they had no idea if this would even be possible. The world was contaminated, there was no doctors and there's no telling how long I would survive if I did come into the world. But it was better than the alternative.

As the months passed, my mother began struggling more and more, trying to adapt to her ever expanding stomach. There were days when she could hardly breathe due to the air being so thin which in turn made my father struggle as he was just trying to keep the 3 of us alive.

Eventually the day of my birth came. A day which parents usually remember and cherish for the rest of their lives. However this wasn't true for my father. My father had a certain amount of medical training but no where near the sort of training required to deliver a baby successfully. And so as my mother went into labour, my father did all he could think of to ensure that both mother and baby would be fine. But it wasn't enough. A complication arose due to the contamination in the air and my mother barely had time to cradle me. She whispered "Blake" just before she passed away. My father tried everything to revive her whilst keeping me alive but it was too much for him and he admitted defeat. He buried her the next day.

So the days, months and years passed until it was my 18th birthday. My father by now had adapted to this new world and I of course had never known any other world. My father's sole purpose in life was then keeping me alive and when the time came, training me to stay alive. As I grew up we had a routine. He was my own personal tutor, he taught me everything from the traditional school lessons like Maths and English, to life lessons like how to survive off of this land and combat lessons. On my 18th birthday we came across a lone wolf hybrid.

"The key is to never attack these in a pack. You must always attack when they are on their own and never let them see you coming" my father said. He would often go out to try and find supplies so in a city the size of what used to be New York City it wasn't hard to regularly come back with an assortment of weapons. He used to always find a variety of knives and the odd occasion he would come back with a gun. He tried to use these sparingly as it wouldn't be long before he ran out of ammunition.

So he began sneaking behind the wolf using boulders as cover. He was clutching one of his favourite knives. A Smith & Wesson tactical police folding knife. At just 4.1 ounces its light enough to make quick jabbing moves but if needed was still able to slit a throat. My father got ever closer to his prey and in a few quick sudden movements the wolf lay still. These were the best lessons I ever received, watching my father first hand take down a beast. My father called me over to help him carry the wolf back to our current home, which used to change often.

"Well at least that's dinner sorted for tonight" he chuckled.I was just about to respond when I caught my fathers eyes. Those dark blue eyes that were just smiling turned serious. I knew something was wrong and so did he. His eyes immediately told me to be deadly quiet. We were both standing still. Both listening intently. I could hear nothing but the shallow sound of my breathing and the subtle wind through the air. The carcass of the wolf laying between us. We were out in the open. We could see the main cluster of buildings in the distance which you would often hear more strange noises from. My dad used to say it was the spirits of all the people that died still going about their daily business in the afterlife.

It felt like an eternity was going by, I just wanted to pick the wolf up and be on our way but I knew my dad knew best and all of his instincts must have been screaming at him to tell him to not move.

A piercing, demented howl ripped through the air. In the distance now we could see more wolves. The rest of the pack. So this one hadn't been travelling alone. And now the rest of the pack had caught up and had seen their fallen comrade and had their deadly eyes fixed on me and my dad.

"Run" my dad said. But I was fixed and couldn't move, I just stared in the distance at the wolves.

"Blake, run!" My dad shouted pulling me out of my stupor. I turned and bolted. Running as fast as I could to the cluster of buildings. My dad did the same leaving our dinner laying on the floor. I didn't turn back. I didn't want to see the pack coming to chase us down. I wanted to see how my dad was doing. As he got older he wasn't as quick as he used to be and neither of us would never be able to outrun the wolves. I was strong and athletic due to my dads training and lessons so stayed in front of my dad. I could practically hear the wolves steps pounding on the ground behind us, making ground on us all the time. The buildings got ever closer, we just had to reach them and we could lose them somewhere. As quick as they were, they wasn't the most clever of beasts. Their brains deteriorating through the years of contamination.

I was practically at the buildings. 15 yards away. 10. Still I waited for some fangs to sink deep into my flesh but it never came. I reached the first building and darted through the door. All the surrounding buildings used to be quaint little houses. Now they stood there derelict, massive cracks running up the side, moss growing from every orifice and covered in dust. But for now they were the safest place. At least I hoped they were. I crashed through the door and darted up the stairs that was on the left and went straight into what used to be a side bedroom to hide and which also had a window to look out on where I just came from to see if the wolves were still there. I was expecting to hear my dad fumbling up the stairs behind me.

But no sound came.

I thought he must have went into another building to try and confuse them and make us harder targets. I crouched down behind a double bed made of oak which was covered in dust. The window was beside me but I daren't look out just yet, just in case they were still prowling. Seconds felt like hours. I thought I left enough time before looking out of the oval window. But it wasn't. I looked down and saw at least two wolves still prowling, circling, trying to pick up the scent of their prey. I ducked straight back down not wanting them to see me and give away my position. A few minutes passed with me living in fear of death coming at any second. I listened to sound of my breathing, the sound of my heart thumping in my chest, working tirelessly pumping blood around my body to deal with the adrenaline I was feeling. I took another glance out of the window. I couldn't see any wolves anymore.

I breathed a huge sigh of relief but didn't get too carried away as they could still be anywhere listening. Waiting for me to make a move. I was just turning from the window, ready to creep out and look for my dad when I saw something. Out where I just ran from there was something on the floor. I couldn't see clearly due to the dust that had settled on the window. I wiped my forearm across the window smearing the dust across the window and getting dust on my clothes. I wiped it once more and the view became clearer.

My heart sank.

There was a body lying on the horizon. The body just stayed in place. Lifeless. There was only one person it could be. Dad.

I went as quickly and as silently as I could. Back through the bedroom door. Tiptoeing down the stairs, looking out for any wolves still skulking about. Halfway down there was a massive creak as I went down the stairs. I immediately held my breath, if there were any wolves still around they would definitely have heard it. Thankfully nothing came. So I continued as quick as I could, straight out the front door. I quickly checked the coast was clear and hastily made my way over to my fathers body.

I reached him and crouched down beside him. I began cradling him.

"Dad! Dad!" I whispered. It was only now I realised I was sobbing. I turned his body over so he could face me. Very faintly I heard his rasping breath. His body moving very steadily up and down and his breaths became less and infrequent. His eyes slid open slowly.

"Blake" he whispered.

"Dad" I exclaimed. "Don't say anything, conserve your energy, I'll get you home".

"No" he rasped. "It's too late, there's nothing you can do". He coughed spewing out blood.

"No" I lied. I knew there was nothing I could do. I had never felt so hopeless. This was the man that had raised me in this hell and against all the odds kept me alive all these years. And now when I had to return the favour, there was nothing I could do except to watch him slip from existence. You could see the damage.

His body ripped to shreds. There was blood all over the ground, all in his matted hair and all over his body. As I examined his body I could see chunks ripped out of his torso, off his legs.

It was hopeless.

"Please dad, don't leave me. You're all I have." I said through the tears.

"You have turned into such an incredible man" he managed a smile through the pain. "Promise me Blake, promise me you will survive for as long as you can, you are more capable than you know. You need to continue looking for anybody else. Promise me Blake".

"I…I promise dad".

"Good". He managed another smile, weaker this time. "If there's one thing I'm proud of. Its you. Through all of this, all this wreckage and death, you're still here. You're a fighter Blake. And remember I will always be next to you fighting alongside you. I love you Blake". His breath faltering and catching. Then his last breath came and he lay still.

He was gone.

Chapter 2

Pack Attack

Another 6 years have passed since that fateful day. I am still here in the same spot. Still living off the land and fending off creatures. Still surviving. I continued training the way my dad taught me, getting stronger, faster, smarter. But there was no one here. No one to speak to, no communication with anybody. It was time to leave.

I carried little, there wasn't much I needed, I had a torch for nightfall along with some spare batteries, a bit of food and water. Other than that it was just the clothes on my back a dagger and a blade. My blade was a beautiful thing. A Crusader sword. 44" with a 35" polished stainless blade and an ABS handle. It had never let me down and cut down many beasts. I started my journey south.

I came through many desolate places. No sign of life, people or demonic creatures. But still I persevered. I knew there had to be life out there. I couldn't be the only one, could I?

Nightfall came. I knew there was no point in carrying on in the dark. Things were a lot harder to see and if any creatures did happen to be roaming about, I would certainly be an easier target. I looked for a place to get some rest. With many of the buildings being destroyed or uninhabitable this could be a hard job in itself. But on the horizon, I could see a building towering above others. I continued my journey to this building.

The closer I got, the more I was dumbfounded by the sheer size of it. It was gargantuan. In all this wasteland, to see a building of this size still relatively intact. It was standing proud whilst other buildings had crumbled and bowed down to it. A couple of the front pillars had crumbled and some showed cracks but on the whole it was still as sturdy as ever.

A sign came into view covered in dust. I wiped the dust and grime off with the back of my sleeve. It read **"welcome to the MET"** and underneath **"Metropolitan Museum of Art"**. So this was the world famous museum my father spoke of. He always said that he was gutted he would never see this building again and that he would never be able to take me. Little did he know he had the opportunity.

The moon was out and shining its light down on me. I thought this was my best opportunity for rest so I took it. I made my way to the entrance. As the wind started to pick up slightly and whip some dust around, stinging my eyes. I stepped into the unknown.

I stood there for about a minute just letting my eyes getting used to the surroundings. I took my torch out and flicked the switch. Its light beaming and bouncing back off of walls. I took in the sheer majesty of the place. Its many great arches demanding my attention, though cracked and crumbling it still was truly a sight to behold. To think that this once could have had 15,000 people and tourist roaming around to now be a playground to filth and bacteria. Contamination everywhere you looked. I began to look for anything I could use for my travels especially food and water.

I went into the many different rooms steeped in ancient history. The many forms art now hanging and standing desolate with no eyes peering on them in a long time. I took my time admiring all the different arts and artists from different countries and different times. I just thought it was a shame my dad wasn't here to talk me through his favourites. I could find no food and drink and thought about retiring for the night but I got a feeling I wasn't alone.

I walked back the way I came, taking more time shining my torches beam everywhere. I had an uneasy feeling in the pit of my stomach. I came out of a room and stood on the balcony of the entrance hall. Again the room showing off just how breathtaking it was. I forgot my light was beaming down as I shined it across the room. Down at the bottom was why I had an uneasy feeling in my stomach.

It was a wolf hybrid and it wasn't alone. I could make out at least four more and they may not be the only ones. And with my light shining down in this otherwise dreary place, all of their eyes fixed straight onto me. I saw all of their mouths widen and show their fangs. A deep rumbling snarl began to emanate from them. They must have came in here looking for food like me. They just found it.

One by one they bounded up the stairs to come looking for me. I had three choices. One I hide, but there was no way I could hide all night just hoping they don't discover me and then it would be easy pickings for them. Two I sneak past them and go back outside. But there's no telling what awaited me out there and if I would find more shelter. Which left just one option. I fight.

But I had to be smart about it, attacking them all together or head on would be foolish. I had to pick my moments and then lash out with my blade. I turned my light off and let my eyes adjust to the darkness, I had no doubt that the wolves eyes were just as adequate as adjusting to darkness as mine but it was better than my torch making me a sitting duck. I ducked back into the room of Greek and Roman art. In the centre of the room there was a table depicting an ancient civilisation of some sort. I hid underneath it. Now I just had to hope that

I could face them one on one and all of them didn't enter.

I waited for two minutes listening to the sound of my breathing and heart trying to even it out and keep as quiet as possible. I was in luck. A lone wolf came wandering in. It began sniffing, searching for any clues as to my whereabouts. It began getting closer to the centre of the room. Sniffing around the different displays and monuments. It got to the table where I was hiding and began sniffing around the feet of the table. I held my breath, not wanting to give away any sound. It was so close, I could smell its putrid breath. The smell of death and decay lingering in the contaminated air. It backed off, maybe smelling the scent of where I once was. I breathed a sigh of relief and realised this was my one chance. I crept out from my hiding place and unsheathed my blade from my back being careful not to make a sound. I used my strength to swing my blade upwards. It cast its demon eyes on me.

But it was too late. The blade cutting through the air and through its neck separating the head from the body. There was a small thump as its body and head hit the floor laying still but other than that, it didn't even have time to give a whimper. One down I thought.

Now to just find the other four whilst hoping they don't find me. I crept to the doorway peering out. The coast was clear as far as I could tell. I tiptoed out of the room. I was in a hallway with doors on either side and one at the end. A sign said Greek and Roman art. I was expecting a mauling at any second, but it never came. I made my way through the door at the end of the hallway and went through a couple more similar rooms. I eventually found myself in the Arts of Africa, Oceania and the Americas part of the museum.

I walked into a room full of more sculptures and different forms of art from the Americas. I saw a huge totem pole standing in the corner of the room, admiring it for a second before a low growl pulled me out of my daydream. I darted behind the totem pole making myself as small as possible. It was the only hiding place I had in the time before another wolf reached me. It came prowling over, once again it caught the scent of me. It knew I was in the room, it just didn't know where. So now it was all about patience, knowing when to strike. Strike too early and it will be ready, strike too late and you miss your opportunity and then the most likely outcome is death.

It got closer to the corner of the room I was in, sniffing all the time. There was no skin or fur around its mouth, just a set of grotesque fangs waiting to sink its teeth into my flesh. It kept getting closer, heading straight for me. It wasn't even turning its head. It was locked onto my position, I was sure of it. In ten yards it would be on me and there was nowhere I could go, nowhere else I could hide. Now only five yards away. 3. 2.

An ear shattering howl broke the sound of my heart thumping. The wolf pricked its head up, turning in the direction of the howl. This was my opportunity. I came out from behind the totem pole and slammed my blade straight through its side and out the other side. I made a wolf skewer. It let out a small yelp but the howl should have masked the noise.

But an almighty bang turned my head on a swivel as another wolf came crashing through the doorway knocking over what was once an invaluable artefact. This time there was no hiding place and its eyes had taken in the situation. There was me standing over one of its brothers with a sword going straight through him. It was angry.

It growled ferociously and began charging at me. My sword was still hilt deep in its brother. I began trying to pry my sword from the lifeless body, but it was no good. It wouldn't budge. It was on me before I could react. Leaping over its fallen comrade, it pounced, landing on top of me. I was underneath the beast doing anything I could to survive. It was snapping and clawing at me. I just had enough strength to hold it off but it wouldn't last for long. Already my energy was draining. It chomped at my arm and I felt a searing pain across the side of my arm. It had ripped a chunk of flesh out but that wasn't enough. It wanted every piece of me devoured. It continued snapping away, saliva flying from its gruesome mouth.

It was getting closer, with the last of my energy, I reached down for my dagger, sheathed on my hip. My left arm, now my good arm, trying to keep it away long enough, while my right arm with a chunk missing, pulling the dagger out and wedging into the wolf's sternum and twisting and burying it deep into its flesh. I wanted to make sure it was dead. It was writhing over the dagger and then it lay still.

I threw the wolf off of me with the help of my good arm and returned the dagger to its sheath. I then went back and twisted and turned my sword eventually breaking it free from the beast. The howl may have concealed the first death but I think the second would have made plenty of noise. And there were still two left, if they wasn't coming this way before, they would be now.

I darted out of the room, making my way through the modern and contemporary arts exhibit, through to the European sculpture and decorative arts, into the Medieval art exhibit and back through to the great hall. The entrance. I was sure the remaining wolves would be following. I needed somewhere to hide. I chose the ticket desk. I crouched behind and awaited any movements or sounds. My left arm clutching my damaged right arm, supporting it.

The last two wolves came hurtling down the

stairs a couple of minutes later. They were hungry for my blood by now, no doubt having seen their brothers defeated. They searched different ends of the room using their noses to try and track my whereabouts. I couldn't risk attacking one when they were that far away from each other. With a damaged arm I wouldn't have been able to withstand the attack from the other. I had to wait until they got closer to the centre of the room. Closer to me.

It was a risky move but I had no other option. I kept peering over the desk, trying to keep an eye on both of them, hoping they don't look up. The monstrous beings drew closer. Now they were surrounding me on both sides. This was it, the final act. It was time to make my move. I drew in a deep breath, trying to ignore my arm screaming in pain and leapt.

I jumped up onto the desk, knowing my actions would make them immediately alert. I then jumped off the desk to my left and brought my sword down with a war cry, plunging it straight through the beasts neck and out the other side. Dead on impact.

The other wolf leapt over the desk preparing to pounce on me as its brother did. But I was prepared. I brought my sword up coming out of one beast and slicing through the next. It didn't have time to react, it just hit the blade and crumpled into two pieces on the floor.

I done it. I defeated a pack of wolf hybrids even though the odds were against me. If only my father could see this. If only he had been alive to witness this feat. I couldn't help but think of him in times like this. But I had to tend to my arm before it got too bad. It was in real danger of getting infected and I didn't even know if they would still have supplies here to tend to a wound such as this.

Then a noise came that I never wanted to hear. A noise that I'm sure would mean the end of me.

The door opened.

Chapter 3

Ray Miller

The door creaked open. A figure was in the doorway. I dived back behind the ticket desk. It wasn't another wolf or any other type of beast. It was a person. Another actual human being. I've never known any other person than my dad and here in front of me was someone else. But the question was: Friend or foe?

I kept my distance, observing this person in the doorway. They were obviously going careful not wanting to encounter any beasts either. I peered over the desk. As the person began creeping forward, I could make out it was a man but nothing more than that yet as it was too dark to see. He looked straight this way.

I darted back down behind the desk. He would have definitely seen the wolves laying dead as well as their fresh blood splattered everywhere.

"Hello" his voice rang out in the emptiness. He had a soft voice with a strange accent I hadn't heard before. It immediately made me want to like him but I knew I couldn't trust anybody.

"If anyone's there I mean you no harm. Not least if you done that to some hybrids" he said. He knew I was there, so there was no use in hiding. I appeared from behind the desk.

"Hi" I replied. My voice sounded strange in the emptiness and as it hadn't had much practice. Now he was closer I could make out more features. He had medium length brown messy hair and dark blue eyes. He looked like he had a handsome face but he was sporting a messy grey stubble on his face. He had a big brown trench coat covering some fitted jeans and a black top. He also wearing black hiking boots.

"You're not hiding from me are ya? I'm 'armless" he said with a wry smile. "The name's Ray Miller". He offered his hand.

"Blake Andrews" I replied and shook his hand. I winced as I extended my arm, forgetting the big gash on the side of it. He noticed as well.

"Christ mate! That's one hell of a chunk taken out of your arm" he exclaimed.

"Oh yeah. Courtesy of one of my friends upstairs."

"There's more?" He asked with a look of surprise on his face. I just nodded.

"I take it he come off worse?" He asked.

"Well it is now laying in a pool of its own blood."

"Good, glad to hear it. Don't meet many people, especially round here." I wondered what he meant by that last comment but before I could ask he continued, "come on, better hope they got something here to clean you up."

We searched around the museum for about 10 minutes before we found a full first aid kit. Ray began cleaning the wound out.

"So what did you mean by you don't meet many people round here?" I asked.

"You mean you don't know?" He responded. The blank look on my face answered his question. "This spot is no mans land. Nobody comes around here because no one ever survives round here. This isn't the only one. There's plenty more around the country and well I guess around the world. Just full of creatures and beasts." There were so many questions swirling round my head but I asked the most important one.

"So if this is no mans land, then does that mean there's places where there are people and civilisation?" Ray was dressing my arm with a bandage but stopped with an amazed look on his face.

"Do you mean to say you've never seen anybody else? Any towns or cities?"

"No" I replied. "I've lived here all my life". At this point, Ray's face turned from an amazed look on his face to a horrified look on his face.

"How the hell have you survived here all these years? All the beasts and creatures?" He asked.

"My dad. He used to be in the army before all this began and he had a lot of expertise in fighting and using weapons and so he taught me how to survive and live off the land."

"Bloody hell mate."

"But you didn't answer my question?" I enquired further.

"You're right I didn't. You're all patched up now lets go and find somewhere more suitable." With that we both began walking through the museum and he began explaining things. Amazing things. He said there were cities and town and villages all over, thriving in this mess.

It was the happiest day of my life. To know I hadn't been surviving for no reason. To know there was still hope for mankind. I asked several questions and he answered as best as he could.

"So what about keeping all the creatures

away?" I asked.

"Well most places have some, we'll call them guards for now, that help fend off any attacks. But to be honest most creatures just stay away from fortified towns and cities. Every so often there will be attacks and some people will die but it's the world we live in now." There was still one question I hadn't asked which I was curious about and I hoped he wouldn't take it the wrong way.

"So Ray, if this is no mans land, what were you doing here?"

"Ah well, I'm just on my way to another place. Grew tired of my old one. Had a lot of bad blood there. Most folks would go the long way around to avoid all this but I can take care of myself so I just cut through" he said. "Anyway, you've asked me a lot of questions, its time I asked you one. You've been here for so long, why haven't you tried to leave?" I stared into distance wondering this myself.

"I don't know is the truth. My dad always used to say we're better off here, we know this territory but if we start going to places we don't know, anything could happen. And after he died, I stayed true to him but I was just leaving and setting up camp here tonight until I was interrupted."

"Okay mate. Well its late" he said with a yawn whilst grabbing his sleeping bag. "We best get some rest for this journey tomorrow. I am assuming you'll be coming with me?" He asked with a smile. At this moment, I couldn't contain my excitement, I had a beaming smile across my face.

"Yeah I would love to" I said.

"Thought you might. Night Blake." Ray settled in for the night in his sleeping bag.

"Night Ray". I laid down on the floor closing my eyes. But sleep was hard to come by at the moment. I was too excited by what tomorrow or the next day might hold. The thought of actually seeing people, seeing civilisation. It all made my head spin. All these thoughts made me drift deeper and deeper until I fell asleep.

*****

I was awoken in the morning by the faint glow of the sun still trying to make its way through the dust and smog. I looked over and Ray wasn't in his sleeping bag anymore. All of his stuff was still there though.

I stood up feeling quite groggy still. I had to wait a moment to let my equilibrium correct itself. I then started to wander out of the room and down the stairs. I caught a whiff of something delicious. I looked over the side and there was Ray in the middle of this massive grand hall with a makeshift stove, made up of splintered wood taken from different places in the building and taken from different sculptures. I continued my way down the stairs and got to the last one before Ray noticed me.

"Ah morning mate". He didn't have to speak very loud as his voice just travelled seamlessly through the air in this open space.

"Good morning" I replied.

"How do you like your wolf steak?" He looked down at the steaks. "Oh. Too late they're already very well done" he said with a smile. It was only now when I glanced over to look at my kills from last night and noticed that the wolves looked like they had been had been stripped. You could see the bones from where Ray had been carving them for food.

"That's okay. Any food will do me the world of good now."

He started serving it up on some plates that I assume he found somewhere in the building along with a knife and a fork. I started tearing at the meat like I was the rabid animal but the truth is I was starving since food wasn't exactly easily accessible all the time. Ray noticed it as well.

"Christ, slow down, you'll give yourself indigestion. Guess you not had food in a while?" Now I thought back to when I did eat and realised I hadn't even bothered eating throughout my journey here. And what with me finding this place, nearly dying and finding out all of the incredible things I did last night, the adrenaline and excitement got me through it.

Suddenly I winced in pain remembering my arm. The bandages had now turned a dark shade of red and were sticky to my arm. Ray had sewn my arm together but something told me it may have reopened during the night.

"We need to have another look at that arm before we go." Before we go was music to my ears. Before we go and meet people. Before we go and live a better life. That's what I told myself.

"So while we finish our food. You have to tell me about your father. He had to have been a special guy, raising you out here and surviving for so long." The thought of him made my heart ache.

"Yeah he was" was all I could reply. But Ray stayed silent and I figured he wanted to hear more. So I talked to him about what my father told me, about my mother and about the sort of guy he was. It was refreshing to hear my voice for so long and tell stories about my dad.

It suddenly occurred to me I didn't even know how old Ray was?

"So Ray how old are you?"

"The big four zero mate." I quickly worked it out.

"You mean you knew the world before all of this." I said not keeping the excitement out of my voice.

"Yup sure did but I'm sure you don't want to hear all that." My face told him to continue.

"Well I was born in a place called Australia." Australia. I'd heard that before from one of my Father's Geography lessons. "From what I can remember it used to be a glorious place. Sun shining, beaches. So much land and not many people populating it. Of course there could be none populating it now." There was a sadness in his eyes and he was quick to move on.

"Anyway I moved to America when I was about 8. 2 years later the world ended. Or nearly anyway. My father died when I was 5. But myself and my mum survived thanks to a public fall out shelter. There's a few dotted around the country. And with that there were people who survived with us and created a little community. So we stayed there until I was 22 when unfortunately my mum passed away. She was beautiful. She had dark auburn hair and brown eyes. At least she was until her illness took hold of her. Funny how even in this world we live, cancer is still probably the biggest killer." Again I sensed a sadness in him. It must have been hard to relive the memory of his mum.

"So I stayed there for another couple of years. This was in Oregon. Then I started a journey east. I visited different places over the years. I went from Oregon, to Idaho, Wyoming, I encountered quite a few beasts there. Then to Nebraska, Iowa, Illinois, Ohio and eventually reached New York and met you." He finished the sentence with a smile. Still looking for a place that feels like home though you know?" He asked rhetorically.

"Right lets clean that wound again and I think it will be about time we set off" he said.

Chapter 4

The Pursuit

He drove a Ducati Scrambler Desert Sled. Its 803 cc engine gliding seamlessly over the rough terrain. He had a smile on his face. He loved the feel of the power the Ducati gave him. This was a man who craved power. Nobody dared cross his path whether they were an enemy or a colleague. He didn't really have friends, they would just tie him down. He thought he was above everyone else and everyone knew it.

His name was Rex Denman. His long black hair seeping out from underneath his helmet. His eyes hidden beneath some goggles to stop the dust whipping into his eyes, were a deep shade of brown. He had a messy stubble that was black but was beginning to grey. And when he smiled he flashed his broken, uneven teeth, souvenirs of his previous encounters.

Rex was at the start of a convoy consisting of 5 vehicles. Two more identical Ducati's on either side of him. He never bothered learning names. Most people end up dead before he had a chance to learn them. He just named these two other riders Tony and Simon.

Simon had long blonde hair and blue eyes while Tony had close cropped brown hair and had a stud in his right ear. Following on from the three riders at the front was two open top Jeep Wranglers with two men sitting in the front and another behind a machine gun mounted turret in the back.

Rex was following some light tyre tracks a vehicle had left the day before. They were fading now with the night air whipping up dust trying to cover the tracks but they were still there. Rex could see a building up ahead. He started bringing his motorbike to a stop and held up a hand to signal to others to do the same. He got off his motorbike and approached a sign. He could see it had recently been wiped down with something and it read ***"welcome to the MET"*** and underneath ***"Metropolitan Museum of Art".***

*****

"So Ray what car did you say this was again?" I enquired.

"Its called a Mercedes. Or a Mercedes Benz S Class Cabriolet to be precise." We left the MET and the mangled bodies of the wolves at 10 am. That was two hours ago.

I walked through the massive doorway of the MET back outside into the chill of the day. Just down the pathway was the most beautiful thing I had ever seen, standing proudly against the background of a barren wasteland was the Mercedes. It was matte black with black tinted windows. Its rims still glistening silver gave the impression that it had been washed recently but I had a feeling it wouldn't last for long. If I thought the outside was good, the inside was better. As I sat in the passengers seat I sunk into the rich leather. I had never known comfort like this in all my life.

"Where did you get this Ray?" I asked.

"Uh, borrowed it" he replied. His answer sounded like there was more of a story behind the answer but for now I let the leather wash away any conversation. Then the engine started. I felt the whole machine spring into life. Everything working together, working as one. Ray began to accelerate, picking up speed. He didn't want to go too fast in this wasteland "just in case" he said. But with nothing else around there was no need. I knew that if we did encounter any beasts, they wouldn't be able to keep up with this machine. I was happy to just cruise. In fact I was the happiest I had ever been in my life. I'd met an actual human, I was on my way to meet some more. Finally a life. Then to further my astonishment, the roof began to fold down and collapse. I looked at it in awe and wonderment.

He explained it was a convertible and spent the next couple of hours teaching me about cars and vehicles but he said there wasn't too many around anymore. You had to be special to have any sort of automobile he said with a smile. Ray had carried on teaching me from where my father left off. I was beginning to think maybe there was a chance at a happy life.

Then I heard it.

Faintly in the distance I could hear a slight rumble. The noise of the Mercedes was doing its best to block the noise but there it was. I glanced down at the speedometer. Ray had taken it to 45 MPH and increasing ever steadily. I looked up at Ray's eyes. The eyes that were usually full of jokes were now serious and in full concentration mode. So he had obviously heard it as well.

I looked in the distance, in every direction searching for the source of the noise. I could see nothing. I checked again and this time, yes on the horizon, I don't know what it was but something was coming and it was coming fast. I glanced back down at the speedometer. Now we were going over 50 MPH. So much for cruising I thought. Ray was keeping his hands steady on the wheel, pushing the accelerator down even more. The sleek Mercedes tearing over the rough, craggy road trying to increase its distance.

But it was failing.

As I glanced behind me again, I could see

whatever this was, was gaining on us rapidly and it wouldn't take too long for them to catch up.

"Uh Ray" I began but the concentration in his eyes cut me off. Instead I just looked back to try and work out the distance between us and what their intentions were. As my eyes adjusted and they got closer, I could make out more details. I could now see a number of vehicles. I tried to work out what they were from the descriptions Ray gave me.

At the front of the pack looked like three motorbikes. These were followed by two open top vehicles and by the looks of it a gun attached to it. I had seen guns before but never had any real chance to see them in action. My father had taught and shown me a little but nothing like this.

This was bad news. I didn't need an explanation to know that Ray and these people were enemies. I'd waited my whole life to see others. Now I have, I'm not sure it was necessarily a good thing. I thought everybody would be like Ray but now I thought I don't even know Ray. This man could be my enemy. He could be leading me to my death. For all I knew the people after him were the good guys. It was in this second I made my decision.

I reached into the back where all of our belongings were. When I got back into the front, Ray was looking at me with bewilderment then understanding. I came back holding a AR-57 semiautomatic Carbine. I found it at the museum and thought it may have been a good idea to bring it along. I just hoped it would serve me better than what I imagined would have happened to the previous owner. I may not know Ray but he was still my first human encounter other than my father and that was enough. Another look at the speedometer showed we had reached about 63 MPH. It took all of Ray's concentration at this speed to keep us going. The defence part would be down to me.

Ray brought the roof back over for the little protection it would give us from the spray of bullets I imagined the machine gun turret would give. I let the automatic window roll down and took aim. I fired a cluster of bullets. All wide of the mark. I had never shot a gun before, let alone one from a vehicle moving at this speed. But it still had an effect, it looked like they didn't expect as much resistance, if any. One of the motorbike drivers swerved at the sound and almost came off but regained his balance. I could just see a tiny bit of blonde hair underneath the helmet. After this they attacked with more ferocity. Two of the motorbikes veering to a side each trying to flank us and the other staying directly behind us. Ray was as focused as ever, keeping the machine at full throttle now, keeping an eye out for any loose pieces of earth or anything that could steer us off course. Luckily there were no buildings standing in this area. I imagined this would have been one of the long routes that connected cities and states.

The faster Ray went just seemed to spur the vehicles following us on. All I wanted was to ask Ray what was going on but his eyes were so full of determination and concentration I didn't want to break it. We had enough problems without me distracting him.

The motorbikes on either side were trying to draw level with us, trying to box us in. I could imagine the flash of light as a spray of bullets hit the side of the car and hit us. The blood pouring out from where the bullets just hit. We had to do something. Ray could see it happening as well but he was calm. The gears and levers working in his brain at maximum. They were still just behind us but the one with blonde hair tried his luck aiming at us. The spray of bullets cannoned into the side of the car just behind my door on the passengers side. It almost cost him. He had to use all his balance to keep upright and stop him from going flailing in the air.

Something told me they wouldn't miss a second time.

They both drew level with us. I might be able to shoot one of them but surely not both. Not before one of them got their shots away and shot either me or Ray. But I had to try. I drew my Carbine out of my window, trying to hold steady and get the perfect shot but swivelling to try and shoot the other guy would be impossible. I turned one last time and looked at Ray.

He was still in complete concentration mode. Just staring at the road in front of him, almost in a daze. But wait. Something had changed. It was ever so slight. But I saw it. Ray had his eyes fully focused on the road but there was an ever so slight shake of the head. So he must have a plan. So once again the question of trust came up. Do I trust him? Or do I try to kill them myself?

My body had already answered as my head was still making its mind up. My arm began drawing in my firearm and rested it on my lap. "I hope you know what you're doing" I thought. I had to fight back the sense of unease and then the sense of urgency as Ray still hadn't begun executing his master plan and the two goons were now either side of us.

"Uh Ray" was all I said.

"You better have your seat belt on" was all he replied. I just had time to double check that it was before I was flung forward or would have been had it not been for the seatbelt, instead the seatbelt dug into my collar bone and chest as it refused to move. Ray had slammed on his brakes just as they were both level, both grinning at each other as if victory was assured. Just as they began firing their guns. Their grins turned into looks of horror as their bullets cannoned into the others body. Both were sent flying.

The guy with the blonde hair was sent flying back with his motorbike losing control and flipping onto its side. The other guy must have got tangled as he lost control of the bike. His helmet came flying off revealing close cropped brown hair with a stud in his right ear. He began cart wheeling over and over again with his bike. Man and machine had become an entangled monster that ended up with the bike on top of the man. A pool of blood already visible to the eye but that was all I had time to see as Ray kept all of his focus on shifting up through the gears as quick as possible to get back to top speed.

The rest of the convoy, that is the last motorbike and two jeeps, all sat back and watched, admiring what was about to happen. They didn't expect to see the Mercedes slam on the brakes and see the other two riders kill each other.

After this they began going full speed, trying to catch up with the Mercedes. The same trick wouldn't work twice. The machine gun's on top of the Jeeps began firing immediately. They weren't taking this lightly anymore. The bullets hit the ground and kicked up dust and rock, followed by mini thuds as they crashed into the back of the car. More shots, more bullets slamming into the Mercedes. This time they wasn't trying to kill us, just trying to blow up the vehicle.

Ray had reached top speed and was in full focus mode. While there was no shooting from the Jeeps, I tried to take my chances and released bullets from my own gun into the Jeeps. This time I connected with their front bumpers and heard a smash as some of the bullets connected with their headlights causing glass to splinter to the floor. It wasn't good enough. They had 10x more bullets than I did and a higher fire rate. I had to come up with a plan to dispose of these Jeeps before they disposed of us. I had to get some good shots away. I took a deep breath, steadied my aim and fired.

Bullseye!

This time my shots connected with the guy behind one of the machine gun turrets. There was a scream and he fell backwards out of the Jeep. He was dead before he hit the floor. At least that's one less problem to worry about. Or so I thought. The guy from the passenger seat climbed out of his window and took up his place behind the machine gun. Immediately he began firing shots. He continued from where the previous guy left as he hit our Mercedes, smashing a brake light. They looked like they meant business now as the Jeep found a new speed. In a couple of minutes it caught up and was side by side with us. The good news is the other Jeep wasn't likely to shoot with the other Jeep so close. I was wrong. Another spray of bullets slamming into the side of our Mercedes caused us to veer into the Jeep alongside us.

The Jeep driver took this as an act of aggression and retaliated by steering back into this. Not to be outdone, Ray steered back into the Jeep. The two drivers were locked in a death grip going back and forth. There was another scream as the guy who climbed behind the machine gun couldn't hold on after Ray smashed into the Jeep. There was a massive rock coming up, Ray saw it and took this opportunity to manoeuvre the Mercedes into controlling the Jeep into the rock. The Jeep driver saw it too late. He cannoned into the rock. There was an explosion and when I looked back the Jeep was engulfed in flames.

The rock was the first sign of things appearing on the horizon as there seemed to be what looked like ruins appearing. Old buildings that had crumbled and fell during the nuclear fallout.

There was just a Jeep and motorbike left. The motorcyclist was still hanging about at the back, clearly hoping that someone else would do the job for him. But now he started attacking with ferocity along with the other Jeep. He had one hand on his motorbike and the other brought up his gun, an Uzi, and let go a couple of rounds of shots. I had to duck down as the spray of bullets smashed the back seat window and glass splintered down in the back seat. Not to be outdone, the Jeep rushed past the Ducati and let off a round of its own machine gun slamming into the side of the Mercedes ruining the beautiful paintwork.

I didn't think we would last too much longer. Ray knew it as well. It was there in his eyes. I leaned out the window to get a better shot. I prayed there wasn't a swathe of bullets that would come and tear me down. There wasn't. I had time to look out the window, take aim and compose myself. At that moment I was entirely in my own zone. Looking down the scope listening to my heart thud. Listening as I took deep breaths composing myself.

I fired off a round from my Carbine and heard a click as I ran out of bullets. Luckily my bullets found their target. They smashed into the front window of the Jeep and hit the driver who lost control of his vehicle. He tried to regain control but it was too late as he smashed into one of the buildings that had appeared narrowly avoiding the last Ducati driver who found a new speed to get out the way of being swatted.

No one would have survived that. Just the last Ducati to go. For most of this battle, he just sat at the back. Watching, waiting, deliberating. Now he was the last one, he attacked with full ferocity. He ripped his helmet from his head and threw it. He was clearly confident he was going to get us. He revealed long black hair and a messy stubble slightly greying. Then he smiled. He knew he had his prey in his sights. As he smiled, he revealed broken uneven teeth. He let off his Uzi continuously not letting up smashing into the paintwork, the interior leather, the brake lights, the windows. Then there was a loud bang as one of the bullets found the rear tyre on my side.

From then everything went slow motion. After the bang I looked at Ray. He was white as a ghost as he lost control of the vehicle. Then the whole world started spinning. With a sickening feeling I realised it was the Mercedes that was spinning. As Ray lost control, it span out and began flipping over numerous times. It was landing on the sides and on the roof. Glass was smashing and the roof was caving in. Something crushed my leg and I let out a roar of pain. The swirling wouldn't stop, I thought I was going to be sick and then we came to a rest upside down. I took deep breaths, forcing myself to stay calm. I looked over at Ray. His eyes were closed. Blood trickling down over his head. I checked to see if he was still breathing. I could see his chest was slowly rising and falling. He was just unconscious.

I had to get out. I unsheathed my dagger, cutting through the seat belt to release me. I tried to crawl out and realised with a sickening feeling, my leg was pinned. What if it was broke. I would never get out and this Mercedes could blow at any second. I was able to wiggle my toes so nothing appeared to be broken. I was just stuck. I yanked at my leg. It wouldn't budge. I kept pulling and pulling trying to fight the rising tension I was feeling.

Then there was a sweet relief as at last my foot came free. I crawled out of the window and was relieved to be out of that machine. "Not a good first drive" I thought. I kept crawling out but I knew I had to try and stand up and go and help Ray. I was just about to try standing when I froze. In all the commotion of trying to escape, I forgot about the person that caused it. It was only when I heard the audible click sound of a gun being cocked that I looked up. A few metres away stood an idle Ducati and a few metres in front of it was a guy with long black hair, brown eyes I could see now his goggles had been removed and a messy stubble that was beginning to grey. He smiled revealing broken, uneven teeth and his hand was holding a gun which was pointing straight at me.

Chapter 5

Wanted: Dead or Alive

"What sort of gun is that Dad?" I asked barely concealing my excitement.

"This son, is a Beretta handgun. Its compact and light making a good choice when you need to be quick." I watched on as he took aim and prepared to fire.

We were in a derelict church. All around us was stained glass windows of Christ and massive pillars that were full of cracks and looked like it was ready to collapse at any second. My dad assured us we were safe.

Bang! Bang! Bang!

He fired off three quick shots and hit all of his targets. His targets this time were three empty tin cans. I was twelve years old and had seen my Dad have several target practices and had never seen him miss. He told me he was a general in the army and its easy to see why he rose through the ranks. He must have been one of the most reliable soldiers. My face had turned from excitement to amazement. He chuckled at the look on my face.

He considered for a moment and then said, "why don't you have a go?"

I couldn't believe it. He was actually handing me a gun. I was going to learn to shoot. My Dad had walked me through what happens but I had never had first hand experience. As I was deep in my thoughts, a sound came that whipped me out of my daydream.

It was a howl.

My dad was next to me straight away.

"Come on, we have to go." I knew it was a wolf hybrid. My dad had told me all about them but I had never really seen one up close. My dad kept me in a lot of the times and only when he had something to teach me did he risk moving me and when we did go out, he was always extra careful. Not careful enough.

We ran over to the doorway. The door had rusted and fell away a long time ago. My dad peered outside and began edging out, bit by bit. I saw him take a look around and then signal for me to follow him. I began creeping out and met my dad outside in the barren wasteland that was New York City.

Another howl came that made mine and my

dads head whip round. In the distance we could see the source. A wolf began bounding towards us and just behind it, more specks appeared and began following. I counted about 5 wolves altogether. We began sprinting in the opposite direction. We just had to get to the underground bunker which we called home which wasn't too far away. I wasn't as fast as my dad was and he knew it so he kept stride with me, trying to protect me. He fired his gun over his shoulder in the general direction of our pursuers. I heard a yelp as a bullet found its mark but neither my dad nor I stopped to look behind. We just carried on running. We were weaving in and out of old buildings trying to break our pursuers line of vision but even if we did, it was likely they would pick up on our scent. We could see the house that hid our bunker in it.

"Blake, get to the bunker and close the door." My father said to which I obliged. I kept running straight into the house and down the ladder which took me into the bunker. I was opening the hatch in the ground and turned just in time to see my dad firing off more shots in the direction of the beasts. He ran out of bullets with a couple of wolves still pursuing. He began sprinting towards me. He fortified the house so we was always protected against such beasts. He reached the house and input a code in the keypad on the wall. Immediately the defence system kicked in. Steel shutters came down over the house and there was a blast of a machine gun as it took out the last remaining pursuers.

I climbed down into the bunker. It was dimly lit with there being no windows, we would often have to go out to get some air. Even if it was contaminated air. The ladder led down into the living quarters and the kitchen. Though the kitchen was used just for what we killed. The living quarters didn't have much either. Just an old sofa, a lamp and a radio my dad would try and use to contact others. He had no luck. We also had books everywhere that my dad had collected before all of this began. Books from a previous life, with everything from encyclopaedias to fantasy novels. With there not being much else to do, I had already read most of them. There was a hallway that lead down to the bathroom, our two bedrooms and a converted study where my dad taught me everything.

This was where we went now. Today's topic seemed to carry on from where we left off outside. The use of guns. He had used many guns before with the army and in this new world. Now he was passing on his knowledge to me. He talked about everything from machine guns, shotguns, handguns to bigger guns like RPG's and anti-aircraft guns though he doubted we would see any of them. Then he pulled out a gun to show me.

"And this Blake is a Desert Eagle." He was holding a small metallic silver handgun. My face didn't look impressed.

"It may be small but its extremely powerful. The recoil will probably knock you off your feet at this age." I reached my hand out to grab it but my dad immediately withdrew it.

"Oh no. This is my favourite gun, I don't even use this. Only for real extreme emergencies" he said.

*****

"Any last words?" the man said. I was lying on the floor, my leg still badly beat up. My whole body felt bruised. I felt like if I was to stand up, I would just collapse into a heap. But in this situation I just stayed still. I racked my brain trying to think of a way out. But I had nothing. I had my sword and my dagger on me but I knew if I even attempted to reach for one, he would shoot me there and then. There wasn't even a rock nearby I could throw to try and protect me. I waited all my life to meet other people and yet it would be another person that would end my life. I recognised the gun he was holding, it had a metallic silver barrel, it was a Desert Eagle. My dads favourite gun.

"No? Sorry it had to be this way. We were only after Ray. He's wanted dead or alive. You're just collateral." He smiled flashing his ugly smile indicating he wasn't sorry at all.

Bang! Bang!

My whole body jumped. Two shots erupted in

the deserted wasteland. I looked down expecting to see my clothes turning crimson. Nothing happened. No pain. No blood. I looked up again. The guy was still standing there but instead of that ugly smile, his mouth was slightly ajar, twisted like he was in pain. Then I saw why. Blood started seeping through the clothes. He crumbled to his knees and fell face first into the dirt.

Behind him, there was a figure standing there with a handgun raised up. The handgun still smoking from being shot and behind the gun was Ray. A surge of relief coursed through me.

"You okay mate?" Ray asked me.

"Yeah thanks to you" I said with a smile. That smile quickly changed to anger.

"Ray what the hell was that about?" I demanded.

"Uh yeah. Sorry about that. Lets grab our stuff and get patched up." He walked over to the upturned car and with difficulty, managed to grab our gear from the back seat which included the first aid kit. He came back over to where I was still sat and tested my leg for any breaks, sprains or dislocations.

"You seem to be alright mate. Just a bit banged up" he said. That was a relief. He then started with the dressing that was still covering the chunk that the wolf took out of me as the old one was now pure red and Ray had to check for any signs of infection.

"So are you going to tell me what that was about?" I asked.

"Yeah I suppose I better" he began. "His name was Rex Denman and he's a mercenary." The look on my face asked for an explanation. "A mercenary is someone who will kill someone for money. For a lot of money and Rex Denman is, well was, one of the most dangerous ones out there. He was known for being one of the most successful but cruel mercenaries. He would always travel as a pack but would send them in first so he wouldn't get his hands bloody. He only did that as a last resort or if he wanted a bit of fun. And if anybody did cross him or confront him from the group, they'd end up dead. He was ruthless." So it looked like I may not have made a good choice siding with Ray. If someone wanted him dead enough to hire a mercenary, he must have done something seriously wrong.

"So why were they after you?" I enquired further. He had finished wrapping my arm up and began to work on himself, starting with his head.

"Well I said I had bad blood in my old town, this was the result. In most places where there is still civilisation, there will be a ruler of some sort. You can call them kings, queens, prime ministers, presidents but we usually just settle for a leader. They're someone who overlooks the town and maintains order so chaos doesn't ensue. My previous town had a leader called Joe Moore. He was an okay leader, people liked him enough and he would listen to the people. But he had a son called Toby Moore and he was as mean as they come. A womaniser, a manipulator and an evil person but to Joe, Toby could do no wrong. He was his only child and the mother had died about seven years ago." At this point he had pretty much finished wrapping himself up in bandages and was just telling the story. He looked deep in thought as he was reliving his past.

"So anyway a couple of months back, there was a rumour. A girl by the name of Maggie Cresswell was apparently assaulted by Toby. Of course Joe didn't believe it. She was brought out in front of the whole town, stripped and beaten. Nobody dared accuse the son of any wrongdoing. And to make matters worse she was banished from the town. And nobody could do anything about it because if they did, they would get the same treatment. And through all of the beating and everything, there was Toby just standing, watching from a distance. And smiling. He was smiling at somebody else's pain." His fists clenched in anger. "Nobody heard from Maggie again." I could see the story getting to him. Tears started appearing in his eyes.

"I never even knew her that well" he continued. "But if we start doing things like that, something monstrous like that, are we any better than the beasts we defend ourselves from?" He questioned.

"Look it's okay Ray if you can't…"

"No you need to hear the full story" he cut me off mid-sentence. He was determined to finish his story. He wiped the tears away from his eyes. "From that moment, nobody trusted the Moore's too much but at the same time, nobody dared defy them or rise against them. So fast forward to about a week ago there was a massive party thrown for the whole town at the Moore's mansion. Well it was more like a castle really. Joe was trying to make friends with the town and get a co-operative relationship going again. The majority of the town showed up, including myself. I had to get food from somewhere." He afforded himself a quick smile before turning serious and continuing with his story.

"It got to about midnight after most had had too much to drink. Out of the corner of my eye, I noticed Toby talking to Myra Pearson. An attractive woman with olive skin, auburn hair and hazel eyes. She was dressed in a sparkling red cocktail dress. He was whispering something in her ear and she was laughing and touching his body. Then they headed upstairs. So I followed. I don't even know why. Maybe it was some instinct. I followed them to Toby's room. They started making out and he started getting really forceful. I could see Myra getting uncomfortable. She said "stop" and he just carried on. Then she said "Toby" and I could hear the panic rising in her voice. This was when he covered her mouth, probably to stop her from screaming. He began tearing her dress off reducing it to a rag on the floor. Images of Maggie in front of the whole town flashed through my head. Myra had given up. You could see it in her eyes. Her makeup had run down her face where she was crying, knowing what was about to happen. I lost it. I stormed into the room, put my hands on his shoulders and threw him across the room. Myra curled up on the bed, trying to get as far away as possible. I walked over to Toby as he was getting up, he swiped his leg and caught me behind the knee so I crumpled to the floor. He picked up a lamp that was on his dresser and hit me round the head with the base. I remember feeling dizzy like I wanted to throw up. Then I started gasping for air." He paused as if he was remembering the pain.

"He had wrapped the cord around my neck trying to strangle me. I was gasping for breath. My head was pounding like my brain was begging for oxygen. I could feel myself passing out. With the last of my strength, I managed to drive my elbow into his stomach. He reeled back winded and fell to the floor. Now we were both gasping for breath for different reasons. He got back to his feet first while I was still on my hands and knees recovering. Then he started running at me looking to pelt me in my head, just in time I recovered and brought myself up to avoid his foot. Then it was my turn I sprinted at him and before he could react I launched into his stomach with my shoulder bringing him down. Then I pinned him down and just saw red. I remember vaguely my fists flying. Repetitively. Right, left, right, left. When I came to my senses again he was still below me but his face was completely red. Covered in blood. Everywhere was. His clothes, my clothes, my fists. I snapped and this was the result. I checked for a pulse to see if he was breathing. He was dead." Ray hadn't changed his expression through the whole story. Just staring blankly in the distance reliving every moment. I could tell what it had done to him. It had changed him.

"I got up" he continued. "I didn't know what to do. I looked at Myra. She was still curled up on the bed weeping. So I ran. Straight out of the castle and then I found Joe Moore's Mercedes. The fastest way to get away. It was open with the key left in there. Nobody would have dared steal from Joe so he didn't need to worry about leaving his key in there. But it was desperate times. So anyway I drove all through the night putting as much distance between me and that town as possible. Eventually I ended up finding you and that's where we are now. I knew there would be consequences. That someone would be coming after me. I just hoped they wouldn't find me but Joe hired the best mercenary there is or was. You just got caught in the middle of it." He had finished his story. I could tell it had taken a lot out of him to relive it. It was a lot for me to take in as well. So that's why there was bad blood in his last town. He had killed someone but that person was an evil man himself. I thought it was best to give him the benefit of the doubt.

"So what's next?" I asked. Ray came out of his stupor.

"We drive on" he nodded in the direction of the abandoned Ducati. Rex wouldn't be needing it now. We finished packing our stuff up and got on the Ducati. Ray driving and me sat behind him. As we drove off, I realised two things. First that there was a lot of evil people in the world. Perhaps that's why my dad decided to shelter me all this time.

And second was that I completely trusted Ray.

Chapter 6

A New Hybrid

We drove until nightfall the first day, then set up camp in some old abandoned building. Ray told me it used to be Charlotte, North Carolina. As soon as the sun rose the next morning we continued our journey south on the Ducati.

"And that's how you get the advantage" Ray finished saying. We were just talking about fighting styles and techniques and what my dad had taught me and what Ray had learned.

"But isn't that fighting dirty, my dad used to say whether you win or lose, just make sure you fight fair" I shouted over the noise of the Ducati.

"Yeah maybe in a competition but this is real life, there's no room for what's fair and what's dirty. There's just winning" Ray replied. I contemplated this for a minute before Ray pulled me from my daydream.

"Oh crap" Ray said. The bike started to slow
.

"What's going on?" I asked.

"Ran out of gas. Looks like we're walking from here on in" he replied. It was about midday as we continued our journey on foot. I didn't know much about where we were going or any places we have gone past but Ray said he's heard good things about a thriving community down south in Florida. We continued on our journey for five hours with nothing but each other for company. Eventually Ray said what I was thinking.

"Do you mind if we stop for a break mate? Bit exhausting, all this walking" he said.

"I was thinking the same thing" I replied. We had stopped outside an old gas station now covered in dust where no one had obviously stepped foot in it for a couple of years. All the petrol and diesel had burned out along with the war. We stepped inside for the bit of shelter it gave. All the shelves were empty from people stealing over the years. Now it was just an empty shop. I noticed something in the corner. Even the smallest of things had not escaped contamination.

"Rats!" Ray exclaimed. He saw my face and realised that even this was new to me. "Horrible little things. Capable of carrying deadly diseases." I looked at them and believed it. Their fur was all patchy, their whiskers all crinkled, their eyes were a deadly shade of green and protruding from their mouth was a pair of long bucktooth teeth. They ended up almost being the size of their body. Ray stamped his foot in their general direction and they scurried away.

"That's a relief" I said.

"Blake don't move" Ray said in an urgent whisper. My senses went on high alert. I thought Ray was looking at me and now I realised he was looking past me. His face was as white as a ghost. All the colour had drained from him. He just continued to stare past me out of the window. I wanted to turn around to see what had him so shaken but I decided to heed his advice. Then whatever it was made a low growling noise and I could hear it shuffle ever so slightly. Again it was like nothing I had ever heard before. It certainly wasn't a wolf and I decided I had to turn around to see what this beast was.

"Blake. No!" Ray said imploring me not to move. I turned around slowly and was met with a horrific sight. Standing in front of me was a monstrous hybrid. Just outside the window looking in was a humongous bear hybrid. I could guess it was a bear from some of the lessons I had with my dad but it wasn't the same thing. This bear was at least seven foot and that was being on all fours. It looked like it may have used to have been a Grizzly Bear but now its brown fur had a red tint all over where years of dried up blood had stained. The eyes were all red and bloodshot and looked like they were hungry for some prey. The claws had grown twice the size and looked like they were developing claws of their own. Inside my heart was racing, thumping as if it was trying to escape my chest.

"Don't move" Ray reiterated. We just stayed there in silence while the bear went about his business. I could just hear my own faltering breath along with the slight shuffle of bear claws. Then the bear got bored and decided to leave. We both breathed a sigh of relief.

"Used to be bears and believe me, you don't want to get into a fight with them. Right lets go". Ray said. We set off to walk outside the gas station.

I sensed it before I even saw it or heard it. If the growl before was scary this one was terrifying. Just as I stepped outside, right around the corner was the bear and it let out a fierce growl that went on for ages. And to make matters worse it rose up so it was on its hind legs. It was easily about fourteen foot now. It had me in its sights. The red bloodshot eyes were staring at me wanting to devour me. I didn't need Ray to tell me. My feet started moving before I even thought about it. I was sprinting as fast as I could away from the beast, hoping Ray was on my trail. I chanced a look over my shoulder to see what was happening behind. I could see Ray just behind me, he must have shot off just as I did. But behind him running at full speed on all fours was the bear. It looked to be covering the distance in no time. It was amazing watching the speed of it.

Of course! I remember my father saying if you run from a bear, it will only make it chase you more. In this instance, the bear is always likely to chase you but running wouldn't help especially since bears are faster than humans. It was then I made my decision. I swivelled and turned around, unsheathing my Crusader sword which was sheathed on my back. Ray wasn't expecting it and nearly ran into me, narrowly sidestepping around me but with the speed he was running at, he tripped and fell, rolling over several times.

"Blake, what the he..." he began but by that point I was running away from him and towards the bear. We were like two gladiators striding towards each other. The beast was preparing to gut me with his claws whilst I prepared my sword to slice through it. I was so close that I could see deep into his red eyes, the smell of his putrid breath filled the air. He brought his claw up to swipe at me. But I was prepared and jumped acrobatically over the claw whilst taking a swipe with my sword. I felt the sweet connection of the blade cutting through the beasts flesh as I landed in a roll back onto my feet. I turned around and saw the beast heading straight back for me. I thought I damaged it but the blade wasn't nearly enough to cut through its thick hide. Made even thicker through contamination.

It seemed quicker than ever as it halved the distance rapidly and was on me just after. It came with its claw again, swiping the air, again I narrowly avoided it by rolling out of harms way. This time Ray came back to help using his own sword, a Katana, to fight the beast. Now it was two on one but the beast still had a massive advantage. The beast squared off against me and Ray. We both stood there swords at the ready waiting for the inevitable attack. The bear came at us swiping left and right, at me and then at Ray. We were both just trying to avoid the swipes. One hit and there would be no getting up from it. He swiped once more at me, I felt his claw cut through the air inches away from my face. But I was ready, I dodged it and brought my blade slicing though the air and through his arm.

At least that was what I intended but as I looked up it had only left a tiny scratch. His skin was near impenetrable.

"What are we meant to do?" I pleaded with Ray for an answer whilst trying to avoid the bears attacks.

"Got to be honest mate. No one has ever survived an encounter like this with these" Ray replied. "The only way people have survived from these is big, big guns but they're all in the towns and cities." We continued evading the beasts attacks whist trying to think of a way to hurt the beast. There had to be a weak point of some sort. Then I remembered something that my father said, his voice still speaking in my ear.

"The key to defeating any animal is knowing the weak spot. Bears weak spot is their nose or snout. Hit them there and they become disoriented." But I didn't want to disorient this bear. I wanted to kill it. I braced myself waiting for its next attack. I looked at Ray and nodded to him as a signal to be ready. Ray ducked under another claw. Then the next one came for me. I leaned back, its claw missing me by inches. Then brought my sword up and back down slicing through the air and then through the flesh of the beast. I hit my target. The beast no longer had a nose as my sword sliced though the snout. The bear was more than disoriented. It was in huge amounts of pain but our job wasn't done yet. This time Ray nodded to me, I dropped my sword. Ray came running at me. I put my hands together locked ready to boost him up. I launched him just as he jumped to gain enough height. He brought his sword round in mid air. The beast still had no idea what was going on because it was still dazed and confused. Ray's sword landed on the beasts neck and continued through it. Severing the head from the body. Ray landed as did the beasts body and then the head. Two parts of the bear just lay there separated from each other. A pool of blood spreading from each part. It was only now I realised how much Ray and I were panting.

"Don't think we could have survived another couple of minutes of that" Ray said breathing heavily.

"Looks like someone has survived one of these attacks now" I said with a smile. Ray smiled back.

"Right then let's get going" Ray said as he picked up his stuff and began walking. I took one last look at the beast. "Hopefully that's the last hybrid I have to face" I thought. Then I began walking after Ray and we continued on our journey.

Chapter 7

Faith Fear

After our encounter with the bear, we continued on foot for a few days, trying to reach Florida in the hope there was the community down there like Ray heard. There wasn't much we could do on these days, other than look out for any more danger, than talk. So we exchanged stories about growing up. Ray talked about what it was like growing up with the war raging on and the after-effects, as horrible and atrocious as it must have been, a part of it must have been fascinating to see humanity evolve right before his very eyes. Then I talked about my dad mainly and all the things he taught me. Every now and then we thought we'd hear something which would alert all of our senses but it ended up being nothing.

    Then I noticed something. Something in the distance. Rising high into the sky. It looked like a massive wall. It must have been at least 50 feet tall with a massive cast iron gate in the middle of it all. This must be it. The moment I've dreamt about. The moment I become part of civilisation.

"Blake, wait" Ray said. I was so in my own world that I wasn't even looking where I was going. I was about to take another step when Ray's warning reached me and I stopped dead in my trap. It was lucky I did as if I took another step, I would never have become part of civilisation as I would have been blown up.

We reached a minefield. Ray had told me the remaining towns and cities protected themselves well against any intruding hybrids. This was just one of them. I could see them now scattered about lots of mines. Any wolves running at speed would never see them and would be blown up and if there were any others following, they would either be killed in the blast or at least be scared off by it. It looked quite secure but I'm sure that wouldn't stop them from having other traps set.

Ray and myself took careful steps in the minefield. Scanning every last square inch of the ground before we took a step. Slowly and carefully we made it across the minefield. When we were sure we had reached the end, we took a deep breath and continued at a faster pace. We cut the distance to the wall in half quickly before we stopped dead in our tracks. Rising from the ground like a phoenix rising from the ashes was a machine gun turret on either side. They both came up ready to cut me and Ray in half.

"No" Ray shouted. As soon as he said it the turrets immediately sank back down into the ground.

"Whew, thank god they're like the ones at the old place. Just needs to hear a human voice to be deactivated" Ray explained. I was still frozen in place, my heart still thumping like mad in fear for my life. Once again I found myself taking a deep breath before continuing on to this gargantuan wall. I was almost scared of any more traps to continue but I put one step in front of the other and continued. Now I was almost at the massive gate, I craned my head up and noticed that all along the walls there were people standing on top. Guards. Guarding against any intruders who happened to make it through the traps.

"That's the guards I spoke of mate" Ray explained again. We reached the massive gate. I wasn't sure what to do now. Just as I was thinking, the gate slowly began creaking open inwards. I felt like I was at heavens gate and it was welcoming me into its arms.

I just saw a slither of what was inside but as it began opening more, I saw more and more wonderful things. Things I only dreamt about for a very long time. The gates had opened fully and I was still so in awe I hadn't moved. Only when Ray nudged me did I begin walking in. The first thing I noticed when I walked in was a massive fountain in the middle of a courtyard. Complete with an angel cherub on top and sparkling, clean water. On either side of me there were houses of various shapes and sizes all decorated differently. Most just plain white outside but some of the houses had flowers and other beautiful things that made the place truly breathtaking. But all of these surroundings were nothing compared to what was beside the fountain. There were a group of five or six children just playing around the water fountain splashing each other. I had never seen children before nor had I seen the next thing I noticed. A woman came out of one of the houses. She looked fairly old and had her grey hair up in a messy bun. She was telling one of the children to get back in for dinner. Something so simple but yet to me so beautiful. We carried on walking in past the children. All around me there were different sights, different smells. Each more pleasant looking or smelling than the next. Someone cooking something wonderful from one house then I looked down and realised there was actual grass on the ground which was recently cut which was a wonderful smell. I could hear children laughing, a baby crying. It truly was like I stepped into heaven.

    Then at once, everything seemed to go silent and even the air itself turned sour. There was no more children laughing. Even the baby stopped crying. There was just the breeze of the wind that interrupted the silence. Then more sound came. The sound of boots marching in unison. I tracked the source to a hoard of official looking people coming towards us. As they got closer, I recognised the uniform as some part of the old U.S army. I remember my dad having similar clothes. "This was going to be some welcome party" I thought. There was about ten men marching towards us. Machine guns thrown over their shoulders. All with straight hats and faces. Business like. Almost like they weren't happy to see us. They stopped about five houses away from us. They turned and went up to a house. Without any warning, they booted the door down and all of them proceeded inside, taking down their machine guns as they did as if they was ready to use them.

No gunfire came. Ray and I just stood there, not sure what to make of it. There was some bangs as a ruckus ensued along with some shouting. Then a guy came flying out of the house landing in the dirt. It wasn't any of the army guys but appeared to be a civilian. He appeared to be Asian with greasy short black hair. His face was already bloodied up but it didn't stop the army guys storming out and beating him some more. There were about five of them just hitting him continuously. Some in the stomach, some punching him round the face. One even stamping on his leg as if he was trying to break it. The other five holding back members of the family. It seemed he was married and had kids and all this was being done in front of them.

"Dad" I heard being shouted.

"Sanjay" the wife said. The five men then carried Sanjay over to the fountain that we saw as we entered the town. Without warning or hesitation, they shoved Sanjay's head beneath the water trying to drown him. You could hear Sanjay's struggles, trying to come up for air and breathe. You could see his family, desperately pleading for them to let him go. Ray and myself had stepped closer to get a better look.

"That's the last time you steal from our leader" I heard one of he guards say. He said it in a standard military voice. Just as it seemed Sanjay was out of time, they lifted his head out of the water. Sanjay came up choking and gasping for breath. But before he even caught his breath, they proceeded to shove his head back under.

"Stop! Stop it!" A woman cried out. It wasn't his wife but instead another woman came into view, rushing over to them. She was the most beautiful thing I had ever seen. She had long, wavy, brunette hair that came down past her shoulders. She had hazel eyes that were full of compassion. She had a slim figure and her skin seemed to have no blemishes. She was wearing ripped jeans and a baby pink tank top with black pumps on. She had me spellbound.

"Please stop it. He's had enough" she had a sweet voice to match the rest of her perfection. The military men took Sanjay's head back out of the water and tossed him to the floor like a piece of garbage. Two of them walked over to her. If this woman was scared, she didn't show it. The two men just smiled at her and walked away.

"Come on men. Lets get back" the head guard said. He was the one doing most of the torturing. All ten of them proceeded to walk away and leave Sanjay be. His family rushed over to him. He was still on the floor, trying to catch his breath. This mysterious and brave woman walked over to the family to see if they were okay. There was a lot of "thank you's" said in her direction. After she saw they were okay and reunited, she began walking away from them and walking towards us.

"Wow! You're one fierce Sheila" Ray commented as she walked past.

"And you two are cowards!" She replied. "And the name's Faith. Not Sheila".

"No, that's not what…" But before Ray could reply she continued walking past us. I thought we needed to defend ourselves, so I chased after her.

"Wait a minute. We're not cowards" I said.

"No? So why didn't you help?" She questioned.

"We've only just got here and we didn't want to make enemies straight away. We didn't even know what that was about." She seemed to consider for a moment.

"Okay. You seem sincere" she finally

decided. "Which is more than I can say for your friend" she continued. I turned around to see Ray trying his luck with another woman and showing off. I smiled to myself.

"Yeah. You get used to him. I think" I said. At this remark she smiled which made me even more spellbound. She had the most beautiful smile to go with everything else.

"Uh Blake. Andrews." I composed myself and offered my hand for her to shake.

"Faith. Fear." She replied and shook my hand.

"Ironic. Faith Fear and yet you showed none then" I said. She blushed. "So what was that about?" I asked.

"From what I gather Sanjay stole a loaf of bread from the leader" she replied.

"And that warranted that punishment?" I asked incredulously.

"That's why I had to try and stop it. It was taken way too far. Sanjay works as a cleaner for the leader and is very poor so he was just trying to feed his family. But the leader is a tyrant. He arrived here about six years ago and has been terrorising the place ever since. He has a personal guard like the ones you just saw. All ex military and all ruthless. If you put a toe out of line where the leader is concerned then there will be some punishment and its never a small punishment."

"Has nobody ever tried to stand up to him?" I asked.

"A few have tried but they've either ended up dead or exiled and most people prefer to put up with his tyranny than face the horrors of what awaits them outside."

"So what does this leader look like?"

"That's probably the most scariest thing. No one knows".

Chapter 8

The Faceless Leader

We spent that evening learning about this town. How it came about, how everybody came together to form this community. It was a peaceful place until the tyrannical leader came and ruined everything.

"But how is it no one has seen him? What about when he arrived?" I questioned.

"He came under the cover of nightfall with his personal bodyguards. The ones that you saw earlier. When everybody woke up, there was an announcement for everybody to meet in the town square and the leader spoke through a speakerphone out of sight and said the old one has been overthrown and that he was the new one" Faith replied. She had taken the time to show Ray and myself around. She then introduced us to one of her friends, Paige O'Connor, who had space for us to sleep tonight. Ray started working his charm on her straight away but she didn't seem interested.

"So what's your story?" Faith asked me. I quickly went through my life, what happened with my father, up to meeting Ray.

"I'm sorry that he was the first person you encountered" Faith said while looking in Ray's direction. Just as she did, Ray began chortling at one of his own jokes while Paige didn't look amused.

"So how old are you?" Faith enquired.

"24. And you?" I replied.

"25" she said. "I still find it hard to believe you're 24 and never left that place".

"Yeah I'm hearing that a lot". A loud knock at the door interrupted the conversation. Faith shot a glance at Paige, who looked back bewildered. Ray and myself were focused and ready for whatever may be behind the door. Paige signalled for us to hide. She opened the door.

"Good evening. We have a message for the people who arrived here earlier today. We have reason to believe they may be here. The message must be delivered to them directly and is from our esteemed leader". It was clearly a guy speaking. He had a deep voice that carried effortlessly through the house and spoke very clearly. Not wanting Paige to get into trouble, myself and Ray went to the front door.

"It's fine" I whispered to Paige. We walked out the front and was greeted by a man in the same uniform as earlier but he wasn't one of the same guards from earlier. He was similar height to me with short brown hair and a thick moustache protruding from his upper lip. Behind him were five guards. All muscular and tall in stature and I recognised some of them from earlier. From the conflict with Sanjay that Faith broke up. This time however there was no machine guns in sight. I had no doubt they would have concealed weapons somewhere amongst them. But at least on the surface they looked like they wanted this to be a friendly message.

"Good evening." He pulled out what looked like a scroll that clearly had something scribbled down on it.

"Our esteemed leader requires the presence of...Your names please?" He asked.

"Blake Andrews".

"Ray Miller mate. Pleasure to make your acquaintance" Ray said in his typically happy way.

"Yes. Well our esteemed leader requires the presence of Blake Andrews and Ray Miller, tomorrow at 3 pm sharp. That is all" he concluded and proceeded to turn around and briskly walk off. He reached the other guards and turned around as if he had forgotten something.

"You'd do well not to hold our leader up. He is not a man you want to upset" he then continued up the roads with the guards. We walked back into the house.

"Well looks like tomorrow, your leader may finally have a face" Ray said. I just stared into the distance wondering what sort of man would run a place like this. I guess tomorrow I would find out.

*****

It was 2 pm the next day. Ray and I had spent the morning out in the community learning more about this beautiful and vibrant place. Vibrant when there was none of the leaders guards about at least. We spoke to different people of different cultures and backgrounds and learned all there is to know about this place since the wall went up to stop any beasts getting in. The same question kept appearing though.

Who is the leader?

It seemed no one knew the answer but now in an hour, hopefully we would. We had just returned for some rest at Paige's house. She said the leaders mansion was on the other side of town and would take a while getting there. With that in mind we set off on our travels heeding the messengers advice last night about not being late. If there was one thing we learned already from this place. It was not to make the leader angry.

"What do you think he wants mate?" Ray asked.

"I don't know" I replied.

"Well whatever it is, I hope there's food. I'm starving." Typical Ray I thought, thinking about his stomach rather than the more important questions.

We travelled for the next 45 minutes. Taking in the scenery and all the people. Well I tried to but my mind was too focused on this upcoming meeting. The mansion came into sight and it was breathtaking. It was set into the wall that protected the town meaning that the back of it was actually situated outside of the town but I thought he must have enough of his private army making sure no beasts infiltrated the place. There were white stone pillars supporting the house with a huge balcony overlooking the town and it was covered in huge windows letting light flood through the house. On the balcony we could see snipers. They were in a rested position but I'm sure they would be ready to strike in an instant if there was a hint of danger. We approached the door and were met by two stern looking men. Again everywhere was army uniforms. I wondered if it was to make people feel safe or scared?

"No weapons allowed" one of the guards said. Ray and I looked at each other and thought it best to not argue. We both relinquished our weapons which included my Crusader sword and Ray's Katana, along with a couple of guns and knives. Surprisingly Ray also pulled out a grenade which I had no idea he had. He noticed my stare.

"For a rainy day" he chuckled. The guards then frisked us down to ensure there were no more concealed weapons. The guards then switched to the other person to ensure the other hadn't made a mistake.

"They're clean" one of the guards spoke in a gruff voice. I realised he must have been speaking to someone inside through a headset because as he said it, two guards opened the door from inside. We stepped inside and felt cool air conditioning on our skin. We were greeted by a woman with shoulder length dark red hair that flicked out at the end and was wearing a long tight fitted black dress.

"Hi. You must be Blake and Ray. Nice to meet you. My name's Karen" she said with a smile and offered out her hand. Both Ray and I shook her hand.

"If you'd like to follow me" Karen said. Ray and myself obliged and began to follow her taking in the sweeping hallways, spiral staircases and grand paintings. With the pace she was going, I didn't have time to take it all in otherwise I would have lost her in this gargantuan place. And I didn't think they was interested in giving a grand tour.

"I do hope you're hungry. Our leader has prepared quite a spread. He didn't know what you'd prefer so he just had the chef prepare a bit of everything." Ray's face visibly lit up upon hearing there will be food.

"And does this leader have a name?" I enquired.

"I'm afraid very few people know that and even fewer have seen him. I myself have done neither and neither will you" Karen replied.

"You mean he won't be there with us? I thought he wanted to meet us?" I enquired further.

"I'm afraid I can't discuss the matter any further." And with that there was no further discussion until we got to the dining room. There was a huge rectangular table that could have seated about 20 people at the table but there was only two place settings. They were opposite each other down the far end of the table clearly intended for me and Ray. Karen signalled for us to go and take a seat and left the room. It was only now I looked around the room and noticed there was armed guards all in the same uniform all with machine guns over their shoulder just like yesterday. A massive painting depicting angels and demons covered one wall. Whilst the wall closest to the table had a huge fireplace with charcoal resting there from the fire the night before. I took my seat facing the fireplace as did Ray opposite me facing the wall with the painting.

Some doors opened and out came some waiters serving a whole variety of foods. There was steaks, eggs, salad, anything and everything seemed to appear in rows of platters in front of our eyes. Once again Ray's eyes lit up and was now licking his lips at the prospect of eating so much food. Even I had to admit to a slight grumbling in my stomach as my eyes witnessed more food than I knew what to do with being served. It still begged the question though: Where was he?

The waiters had finished serving the food and had left just the two of us and the armed guards. Just as they left, I heard an electronic whir. I looked to my right at the wall and Ray looked to his left and was amazed to see the wall separating from each other. Slowly edging further away from each other. Behind the wall was massive TV that ran from the floor to the ceiling. Ray and I exchanged glances not sure what to think or do. Then the screen flickered and turned on.

There was a silhouette of a man. But that's all it was. He was shrouded in darkness so he didn't give any features away. Looks like we wasn't going to meet the leader today.

"Good evening. You must be Blake and Ray" he spoke through a voice synthesiser to make it seem really deep so even his voice isn't recognisable.

"I'm Blake and this is Ray. And your name is?" I spoke up after a few seconds of silence.

"You can just call me the leader" he replied. He really wasn't giving anything away. All you could see was a vague outline, his voice was distorted and he wouldn't even give his name away. I'd had enough.

"What's with all the secrecy? Why hasn't anybody seen you or know anything about you?" I burst out. Within seconds the atmosphere in the room changed. All the guards were suddenly focused on me, they now were cradling their machine guns. The leader held a hand up and all the guards relaxed and assumed their previous positions.

"You are a guest in my town. You'll do well to remember that. Now what business do you have here?" He asked. This time Ray spoke up, afraid of me having another outburst.

"We're just looking for another place to stay, I couldn't stay in my old place and Blake definitely couldn't stay in his old place and I heard good things about this town. So we decided to come here and become part of this wonderful community." I could tell Ray was sucking up a bit to try and make up for my outburst.

"First I want to hear about your backgrounds and how it is you have reached this destination. And please don't let the food go to waste" he said. Ray didn't need to be told twice as he got stuck in to all the different types of food that had been laid before us. I began telling my story, of how my dad raised me and how I survived. Then when I had finished Ray told his story whilst I got stuck into the food and I had to admit it was marvellous. I had never had a feast like it. Ray finished telling his story but left out the part of why he left his last place. Again bad blood was all he said. It was now silent while we waited to hear from the leader. He seemed to be deliberating on a decision.

"Fine" he eventually said. "I will allow you to stay but I don't have any slackers in my town. If you stay, you have to pull your weight. Is that understood?" Me and Ray couldn't help but feeling like we were getting told off by a parent or teacher the way he spoke to us. He reminded me of the way my dad used to speak to me whenever he was warning me about something. We both nodded our heads.

"Good. I'm glad we understand each other. Karen will show you out and will let you know what jobs you will have" the leader said. Karen was there by our side as soon as he had finished and began escorting us out. I looked back at the TV but he was already gone as would the TV be in a couple of seconds as the wall began to slide back into place.

I came into the meeting thinking I would have more answers but it just left me with more questions. Why was he so determined to not let anyone see him? Why does he have a private army at his command? What happened to the old leader if he just appeared in the middle of the night? But still there was one good thing that came out of it.

I now knew how to infiltrate the mansion.

Chapter 9

The Masquerade Ball

"I don't wanna do it" Ray said.

"Look I'm sure it's not that bad when you get into it" I replied.

"That's easy for you to say, you don't have to do it. Why couldn't they have given me a job with you? Or a fireman?" It was a few days after our meeting and Karen had given us our jobs as the leader said she would. I'd been given the job of being a guard, protecting the people from any intruders. Ray wasn't quite so fortunate. He'd been given the job of a farmer. This meant he was responsible for growing all different types of fruit and vegetables. He did learn how this was possible on his first day. They explained that they had decontaminated the land when they first settled here meaning they could grow things but Ray being Ray zoned out for most of it. After a few days, he was already tired of it and was annoyed at me because of my job. The day was Saturday and it was the day to put our plan into action. The day to infiltrate the mansion.

"So you know what you're doing?" I asked.

"Yeah, yeah leave it to me" Ray replied.

"Remember Ray you get caught, we'll be on the run again. Or dead" I added.

"Thanks for the vote of confidence mate. I'll see you later" Ray replied. Then he winked and left. The plan came to me when we had our meeting. Right in front of my eyes, a way to infiltrate the most guarded place around.

A ball.

There was a massive banner up saying 'Welcome to the 6th annual masquerade ball', in preparation for tonight. As soon as we got back, I asked Paige and Faith about it and they said it had become a huge hit in a short space of time and now it was the biggest event of the year. But only if you're firmly behind the leader. It's a place for all the stuck up people that the leader looks out for whilst the others slave away to help the town. So I told them that was how we get into the place. At first they all refused, but eventually I convinced them to help and so we set about making a plan.

Paige is a cleaner for some of the leaders supporters and had already seen some masks to disguise ourselves with and was going to hand off the masks to Faith who had the "perfect hiding place" she said. Faith was then going to secure some clothes for us to wear so we could blend in.

Faith happened to be involved in the fashion in this town. Then it was up to Ray to actually secure the tickets. The people who were in charge of farming were a couple of brothers and they had wives so he was going to steal four tickets for us. As for me, I was on wall duty so there wasn't much I could do as if I even thought about abandoning my post there would be a full inquest and I would never be able to complete the mission.

Paige and Faith were in the corner going over their part of the plan for the trillionth time.

"You two know what you're doing?" I asked.

"Yeah don't worry, you take it easy. Leave the real work to us" Faith joked. I smiled.

"Remember any sign of trouble, leave it, it's not worth it. I wouldn't want anything to happen to you" I realised I was staring at faith.

"Either of you" I added. And with that I said my goodbyes and wished them luck. Now for me it was just a waiting game, I just had to hope that each of them would succeed in their missions.

I just had to have faith.

*****

The day dragged on. Waiting, watching. The sun behind the smog rising and falling. Every so often, you would have to be alert and something scurried by in the far distance but it's as everyone has said, any beasts just stayed away. For my first couple of days I had tried making conversation with my colleagues but it was no good. They kept conversation to a minimum, preferring to stay fully alert. I would have loved for Ray to be here just to hear my own voice but still I had got used to it always being silent around me after my dad died. It was creeping into the evening and the second lot of guards would soon replace us, taking the night shift. Now I was getting impatient to get away.

Finally, I saw the first lot of new guards coming preparing to replace them. There was a rule that you wasn't allowed to leave your post until the new ones were there so I didn't want to draw any attention to myself. They began taking their positions so I went as quick as I could not trying to make it obvious I was eager to get away. I almost slid on the ladder to get down from the protective wall that enclosed the town. Then I broke into a half run, half fast walk. I got to Paige's house in half the time it usually takes me. This was where we all agreed to meet. The door flew open in my eagerness.

No one was home.

"Ray, Faith, Paige" I called out. There was no answer. Something had gone wrong. They must have been caught or worse.

"Oh hello mate." The voice came from

behind me in the doorway. I was relieved to see it was Ray.

"Where were you? Did you get them?" I asked. He pulled out something from behind his back and flashed the tickets.

"No worries mate. Just hope they don't know it was me" Ray said.

"What about Paige and Faith?" I asked. Suddenly Rays face turned sombre.

"Haven't seen or heard from them yet. But I'm sure they'll turn up". They should have been back by now. We agreed to meet back here at 6 to get ready and go over the final preparations and then leave about 7. As the minutes crept by I was getting more anxious. Something had gone wrong. It was already 7pm and people would start arriving at the mansion. Then the door crashed open. It was Paige.

She was panting and sweating slightly and had something slung over her arms. I then recognised them as our clothes for tonight. But there was no Faith behind her. This time my face turned sombre.

"Where's Faith? I asked.

"She's fine. We ran into a bit of trouble and she decided it best not to be seen together and she will meet us at the party" Paige replied. I breathed a huge sigh of relief. I was beginning to suspect the worst.

"What about her ticket?" I then asked.

"That's taken care of as well" Paige replied.

"We'd better get moving. We're already late" Ray said. I nodded and we all began getting ready as quick as we could. It was a new style for me. I had never needed to be dressed so formally and struggled a little bit with my tuxedo making sure I looked the part. Ray had to help me a bit and took great pride in mocking me. We both were finally ready and put our masks on.

"Looking good mate" Ray said.

"You too" I replied with a smile. We had got ready downstairs in the living room and just as we had finished Paige came down. She was dressed in a long, dark blue shimmering satin dress complete with blue high heels. Her long black hair straightened.

"Wow" we both said. She smiled.

"We had better leave" she said. She was right. It was now 7 30 and we wouldn't get there till gone 8 which was already less time than I was hoping for. Paige put on her blue mask to match her dress and left with us.

The journey there was spent by me

worrying about everything. Was Faith ok? Will we get in without any problems? Will our plan work out? And in the background I heard Ray paying Paige compliment after compliment whilst she was rejecting his advances.

We finally reached the mansion and if there was a lot of guards before, there was 10x the amount now. I had never seen so much security in one place. You wouldn't be able to turn the corner without seeing a guard. This was going to be a lot harder than I thought.

There wasn't many people around since most would be inside already. Just a couple of groups filtering through.

"Right are we ready?" I asked. They both nodded unconvincingly obviously coming to the same conclusion that I did. We hurried forward to join onto the end of a group already going in. Each presenting their ticket before getting thoroughly searched. We had already agreed not to bring any weapons as we knew we would be getting searched and thought it better not to take any risks. We would just have to hope that we wouldn't need them.

It was our turn to enter. I was at the front and presented my ticket which the guard scanned thoroughly looking for anything out of place. He waved me forward to be searched by a second guard. He searched me for what seemed like hours like he was determined to find something. Then he stood up and looked at me. He nodded and let me through. My whole body wanted to jump for joy at successfully making it in but I kept calm and carried on walking through.

"Excuse me sir" one of the guards called out and I stopped dead in my tracks. Looks like I started celebrating too early. I had been caught, they're going to lock me up or kill me. I turned around.

"You forgot your ticket. You need to keep it on you all night just in case there are any random searches" the guard said and went back. I breathed a huge sigh of relief just as Paige was let through and then after a minute Ray was. We made it through without a hitch. "So far. So good" I thought. We went back through the halls we had travelled in just a few days before but instead of going to the dining room as before we were directed to the ballroom just down the hall. We entered and was astonished to see such a sight. It was beautiful. It was a marble floor with white walls all around. On the walls were various paintings and portraits of different times and eras. In the middle, dangling from the ceiling was a huge chandelier glistening. At the back was a grand staircase that went left and right, there were people all along the staircase and at top, both left and right. Then on the floor again, dozens of people all dressed in beautiful dresses and fancy suits all adorning a mask of some sort and sipping champagne. All around the room, just as before were guards all wearing the same uniform, keeping an eye on proceedings. We took a step forward and were immediately greeted by a waiter carrying a tray of champagne. He had brown hair which had been slicked back and combed down, he had a thin, wispy moustache and blue eyes. And he was wearing a pristine white shirt and black trousers with a black waistcoat over the shirt. I looked down and saw he was wearing black shoes that had been polished so much, you could almost see your reflection in them.

"Champagne?" He asked in an unnatural voice. We all took a glass. Ray as usual was over eager to get his hands on a glass and downed it straight away and gave the glass back to the waiter. Paige took a more relaxed approach and sipped it slowly. I have never experienced any alcohol before and sipped it. Immediately I wasn't a fan and my face showed it. Ray laughed and I handed it to him. He downed it straight away again and set the glass down on a table. We started walking to the centre of the room to try and get a feel for the place. Faith still hadn't made an appearance. I began to scan the room looking for any sign of her but there was nothing. I was starting to panic.

"Wow!" I heard Ray exclaim. Suddenly it seemed as if the whole room went quiet and was staring at one place. I followed their eyes and where Ray was looking in awe. At the top of the stairs on the left hand side was an absolutely stunning woman. She was wearing a long ruby red cocktail dress, pleated at the bottom. She had red strapped high heels complete with red toenails. Her hair was brunette and curled to perfection. And in her ears you could see a shimmer of a diamond set in place. Red lipstick had been delicately placed on her lips. She was finished of with a shimmering red mask that covered her face but could see her beautiful hazel eyes through the slits. She made her way to the bottom of the staircase and began to make her way over to us.

She was breathtaking.

Then realisation came. It was Faith.

"Wow, what an entrance" Ray said.

"You look beautiful" Paige said.

"Thanks. So do you" Faith replied. Then she started looking at me. I was speechless. I tried to think of something to say but no words came. She looked a little disappointed but quickly shook it off.

"You clean up nice" she said.

"Yeah you too" was all I could manage to say. A slow song started playing.

"Oh I love this song" Ray said and before Paige had a choice, she was whisked off to find a place to dance. That just left me and Faith. I had never had any experience before in these situations so I went with my gut instinct.

"Shall we?" I asked whilst extending my hand out to her. She smiled and then took my hand. My limited experience with dance told me the man was supposed to take the lead but Faith was walking me through it. After getting the hands in the right place, we began dancing.

"Ouch!" Faith exclaimed.

"Oh, sorry" I apologised after standing on her feet a couple of times.

"Its fine. Just relax" she said and then she gave me a smile. Her smile made my heart skip a beat. Being so close to her made me realise how much I underestimated how beautiful she was. She also smelled incredible. It was the sweetest scent I had ever smelled. She truly was breathtaking and her smile made me relax. I was completely entranced with her.

We began flowing in time with the music. I was wondering what she was thinking as she was staring into my eyes. Her beautiful hazel eyes looking into mine. She looked away and when she turned back, her eyes had become serious.

"You see that guy over my shoulder?" She asked in a whisper as we continued dancing. I peered over her shoulder and saw another guard but not like any other guard. He was different. It was similar in uniform but it looked like a higher ranking officials uniform. His muscles were bulging so much through the uniform, I thought they were just going to tear straight through. He had a crater face and blonde, flat top hairstyle. His blue eyes were just watching over the proceedings, looking out for any sign of trouble. I nodded.

"That's Henrich Schroeder. He's the head of security for the leader and he is as mean as they come. If there's any particularly horrible business that needs attending to, he's the one they turn to. He's one person that you might want to avoid" Faith said.

"Noted" I replied. Henrich then walked off somewhere just as the music stopped and a voice I recognised as Karen's played through some speakers.

"And now it is my great honour and privilege to introduce our esteemed leader" she said just as a screen emerged showing the same picture Ray and myself saw when we had our meeting and applause erupted all around us. We thought it best to join in so began clapping just as Ray and Paige joined us again.

"Thank you. Thank you all and welcome to the 6th annual masquerade ball" and more applause erupted around the room. His voice was again distorted, giving nothing away.

"Another year has gone under my leadership and things have never been better. The land is thriving, people are living well and we have had no beasts try to infiltrate our walls in six months". Again more applause broke out. It seemed everybody was extremely eager to applaud him at any point. I noticed everybody was giving him their full attention. I tugged on Faith's hand to let her know it was time to put the plan into action and then nodded at Ray to let him know. Ray and Paige were going to stay here and be distractions should anything happen whilst Faith and myself was going to check the place to see if we could find anything.

We walked back out the way we had come, there were still guards posted around so we had to be careful. A couple walked past and Faith pretended to laugh at an imaginary joke I told. I thought it may be worth checking out the dining room for any clues. I looked down the hall to see if it was clear. It was so we started to venture down the hall. Most guards seemed to be posted in the ballroom.

All of a sudden a guard came out of a door I hadn't seen before and turned towards us. In the same moment, I felt myself being pushed against the wall and Faith planted her lips on mine. Butterflies erupted in my stomach. It was magical, I sank into the kiss and just as I really started to enjoy it, she backed away.

"He's gone. Sorry about that" Faith said. I realised it was so the guard didn't ask any questions. As far as he was concerned we had just slipped away from the party to have a little alone time.

"No. It's. Fine" I said but it came out in three sentences whilst I was still trying to get my breath back and stop my heart from racing. Faith smiled and walked on towards the dining room. We got to the dining room and peeked inside to check for any guards. It was clear and so proceeded inside. This was just where we were a few days before. This time without guards watching my every move.

"Wow" Faith said as she looked around taking in her surroundings.

"Right lets start looking for anything unusual. And lets be quick about it" I said. We began searching. Looking in every corner turning every object but it was no good. Faith was over by the fireplace and was admiring a candelabra that was on the mantelpiece above the fireplace and then there was a sudden whirring sound similar to the sound I heard before when the walls separated.

"What did you do?" I asked.

"Nothing" she replied. It wasn't the same wall as last time. This time I noticed in the fireplace, the wall behind slid open. There was a secret entrance in the fireplace. I was amazed by the technology but I didn't have time to admire it for long as we heard voices and they were getting closer. There was only one place to go.

"Quick" I said. Faith ducked down and crawled through the fireplace, with me just behind her. The secret entrance then concealed itself again. Just as it closed an I thought we was going to have to do this in the dark. Light illuminated the dank and dreary passage. It showed a long sweeping stairwell. We couldn't see the bottom. We started our descent going deeper and deeper underground into the depths of the mansion. The walls looked all slimy and had moss growing out from them. We reached the bottom eventually and was faced with a long corridor. We heard a scream. It sounded like a man.

"What was that?" Faith asked.

"I don't know. But we have to find out" I replied. More screams. It sounded like he was in a lot of pain. Down the end I noticed a desk with a chair behind it and had to stop suddenly. Thankfully, it was empty. I was sure there would usually be a guard behind it but he was probably the one causing the screams. This was just a short passageway and at the end, I could see more stairs. There was a row of cells on the left which just had one door fixed into the wall. It looked to be made of iron and just had a little window in the front with bars across it. It was a prison. The screams seemed to be coming from the second cell in.

Slowly we edged over to it, creeping slowly and silently although I was sure the screams would drown out any noise we made. We reached the door and peered inside. I could see two men in there. One I didn't recognise. He looked old and haggard. He had grey hair that looked like it hadn't been cut for years and came down past his shoulders. His beard matched the hair and his face looked like it had been worn out. The other guy I recognised from seeing just a few minutes before. The bulging muscles, the blonde flat top. It was Henrich. And he was clearly torturing this man. He looked to be electrocuting him with some sort of device, causing him to scream out when he did.

"What do you see?" Faith asked.

"Henrich torturing someone but I don't recognise the other man" I replied in a whisper.

"Let me see" Faith said. I obliged and stepped out of the way for her to look. She appeared to be there for a few minutes and then she turned back with an odd expression on her face. She looked like she recognised the man. She looked like she had seen a ghost.

Chapter 10

The Assassination

A few days had passed since we infiltrated the mansion. After we looked inside the prison we decided we had seen enough. We left the mansion, thinking going back the way we came in would be easiest route since we didn't know any other route or what guards lurk around. When we reached the fireplace, we realised we didn't know how to open it this side and if anybody was waiting on the other side. As we approached the concealed entrance, the fireplace opened back up anyway clearly having motion sensors built in somewhere. Thankfully, there was no one on the other side either, we made our way back towards the ballroom to rejoin Ray and Paige.

Faith barely said anything to anyone and I didn't want to press the issue and make her more upset but I had to know who the guy being tortured was. She clearly knew him. I was coming to the end of another shift on the wall and was hoping for some answers tonight. Ray and myself were still staying at Paige's for the time being and Faith was there more than she was at her own house. The other guards came to relieve us of our duty and as usual I rushed off as quick as I could much preferring to be with Faith. By now I knew the quickest way back and so didn't take me long before I was at Paige's house. I opened the door and saw Faith and Paige talking on the sofa. Faith looked up and smiled at me.

"Hey" she said.

"Hey" I replied. I was just standing there admiring her beauty when Ray barged past me and brought me back to earth.

"Hello mate. Hope I didn't distract you" he said with a wink.

"I'm glad you're both home actually as we need to speak about the other night" Faith said. It looked like she was finally ready to reveal who the guy getting tortured was. Ray and myself both took a seat. She took a deep breath and began.

"Remember we said that the previous leader just disappeared in the night and this new one took over?" She asked rhetorically but I felt myself nodding anyway.

"Well we found him" Faith said. Suddenly it all clicked, the guy getting tortured was the leader and he hadn't disappeared. He had been in the mansion all this time getting tortured.

"So he's the guy you saw?" Ray asked. Faith just nodded. She had already told Paige as she didn't look surprised just had a sombre look on her face.

"So what are we going to do? We need to tell someone" Ray said answering his own question.

"Who can we tell? That tyrant is the one keeping Marcus hostage and torturing him. There is no one to tell" Paige said. So Marcus was the previous leaders name. We all knew she was right. We couldn't say anything to anyone, no one would believe us and if anybody did, they'd end up dead or banished from the community. I had an idea in my head but I didn't want to say it out loud and make it real. It was too risky but it may be the only thing we can do.

"We need to infiltrate the mansion again" I said. There was a minutes silence. Then Ray laughed.

"You're joking right? How could we possibly do that alone? The only reason it worked first time is because of the ball and even then we were lucky" Ray said. He had a point. The first time was sheer, dumb luck but try it again without the cover of a party, I'm not sure we would be so successful. But we couldn't not do anything.

"We have to try" was all I said. The words

seem to hang in the air as if everybody was really digesting what I just said.

"I'm in" Faith suddenly popped up and said. She gave her beautiful smile again and I smiled back.

"Me too" Paige said.

"Well I guess I will as well. Can't have you lot messing it up" Ray said.

I smiled thinking that not long ago, the only other person I knew was my father.

I smiled knowing we were about to rescue another person being held captive by another person.

And I smiled knowing that I had three amazing friends.

*****

It was another day on the wall. Waiting impatiently for the new guards to show. I had spent all day visualising the infiltration and every time we had been caught. I tried not to think about it but my mind kept working on it. Tonight we was going to scope the place out. Have a look for the best point of entry and see what time the guards change. Anything we could to give us an advantage. The new guards had turned up and as usual, I wasted no time getting away, eager to get back to Paige's.

I took my usual route passing various houses and workplaces. Passing society.

Suddenly I heard a noise. It sounded like a person crying and in distress. I stopped in my tracks. The noise continued. I looked around but there was no one else around. The noise was coming from in between two tall buildings. Clearly factories of some kind. I looked down the alley and there was a person crying on the floor in a heap. I couldn't tell if it was man, woman or child by the way they were on the floor and they had a hood covering their face. There were two big commercial bins on either side.

"Hello" I called down there. It was quite dark and could only just make out the outline of the figure crying.

"Help!" Was all I heard them respond through the crying. I couldn't just leave them so I walked down this dark alleyway taking my time. The crying intensified and so did my speed. I was just walking past the bin as the figure looked up.

Suddenly I was sent flying through the air and came crashing down hard against the brick wall on the other side. Someone or something had hit me. Hard. I was dazed and confused. My whole body rocking. I tasted blood instantly in my mouth. I had landed in front of what looked like a fire exit door. I could just about make out that the person crying had disappeared and instead was replaced by this behemoth of a man. I couldn't see his face as he had a mask covering it. But I knew that I had walked into a trap and was in terrible danger. He came at me again, this time with his knee ready to slam into my chest and knock me against the door. I just had enough time to react and managed to roll out of the way. I heard the slam of the knee into the door and when I turned back round, he didn't even look hurt but instead there was a massive dent in the door. This person wasn't ordinary. I got to my feet and charged as best as I could at him but he was too quick and sidestepped me easily. I just had time to turn back around before once again I was lifted of my feet. He had me in his arms and still charging. I felt myself crash through something and natural light turned into artificial.

Then I was on the floor. He knocked me through the fire exit door into the building. I saw some metal steps leading upwards and another door behind me. Once again he was on me before I had time to react. This time he threw me up the stairs but I started to roll back down and was met with a swift kick to the ribs knocking all the wind out of me. I was struggling to breathe. But that didn't stop him picking me up to my feet and drag me to the top of the first flight of stairs and threw me against the wall. I came crashing down to the floor again. I was in real danger now. If I didn't escape from him somehow, it would be over. Out of the corner of my eye I saw something red. I recognised it as a fire extinguisher. Sensing my opportunity I quickly stumbled to where it was. I managed to get it off of the wall but before I could do anything, my head once again slammed into the wall. I touched the side of my head. When I looked at my hand, it was soaked with blood as was the wall where my head connected with. It was now or never. I had to get away.

I reached down to my hip and just managed to get a hold of my dagger just as he began his next attack. I could tell he was having fun but that was about to end. As he grabbed hold of me, I swung my dagger down and planted it straight into his foot. He shouted in pain but he released me and stumbled back a bit. This was my opportunity. I sensed it. I picked the fire extinguisher up again and rammed it straight into his stomach. This time he was winded. I went for the killer blow to his head but as I went to, my legs gave way. My body had failed me from all the blows it had already taken. I did the next best thing and sprayed the fire extinguisher. Foam erupted out of it straight into the other guys face, blinding him and enraging him more but it was enough. I managed to stumble away, up the stairs and tried to recover as much as I could. I took the stairs all the way to the top and crashed through the door. I came into a factory of some sort. I was on a single walkway stretching from one side to the next. On the other side was a door that looked like it led to the roof. Below was lots of advanced equipment I couldn't possibly understand along with various vats of chemicals.

Each one looking more dangerous than the next.

The throbbing pain in my head brought me back to reality. How long till he found me? I didn't know how long I blinded him for or how long he would take to find me. I got my answer instantaneously as the door swung open again and there he stood. But this time his mask had been removed, probably from the foam getting in his face, and I recognised him. I had seen him just a few days earlier.

It was Henrich. No wonder he had busted me up so badly already, the muscles weren't just for show. Now he had a sick twisted smile on his face which along with the bloodshot, red eyes made him look crazy. He began slowly walking over to me. Like a predator stalking his prey. I had recovered slightly and got my breath back but my whole body was still aching from the onslaught I received earlier. He edged closer to me. I was gathering all the strength I could.

"Stop. Why are you doing this?" I asked. I hoped it would do any of three things. One: give me an answer. Two: give me more time to recover. Three: distract him. It didn't work. He just snarled and continued. Then he rushed at me. There wasn't any room to sidestep so I had to try something so risky that one mistake and I'd be dead.

As he was nearly on top of me, I grabbed hold of the side and swung myself over. For a second I was in midair flying over the chemicals but my hands were holding onto the sides with all my strength and they brought me back, clinging to the side like a spider. Henrich must have looked so surprised that he wasn't paying attention and fell over himself cracking his head against the side. The impact rocked the walkway and I felt it wobble underneath me while I was still clinging on for my life. I managed to hold on and bring myself back over but Henrich was already back on his feet and looking for his next attack. It seemed impossible to keep this guy down.

He came at me with his fist, swinging with his right. I narrowly avoided it by ducking down. Then came his left looking to connect with my chin but I stepped back and avoided it. I saw an opening and attempted a straight kick to his chin.

I felt the sweet connection of my foot hitting his chin.

Henrich didn't move. He just smiled like he didn't even feel it and now it was his turn. Quicker than I thought was possible, he done a straight jab to my chest which sent me through the air, landing five feet away from him. Again pain coursed through my body. I needed to do something and quick otherwise I wouldn't be walking out of here. Again Henrich moved with lightning speed. I came to rest against the side of the walkway. Henrich was already on me and launched his foot, heel first, towards my head. Luckily I moved to the right and avoided it but then there was nothing to lean against. With a sickening feeling I realised he had kicked the side clean off. I heard the clatter of the support bar hit the floor beneath us. Now I had nothing behind me supporting me, protecting me from falling to my death. Henrich was on top of me, trying to push me off to my death. I was doing everything I could to resist but with his strength, it wouldn't take long for him to get the better of me. My resistance began getting weaker by the second and I knew this was the end.

"If only your father could see how weak you had become" Henrich said in a thick accent not from this country. Two things happened. First was complete shock from me at him mentioning my father. And second was a sudden surge of strength that coursed through my whole body at him mentioning how weak I was. I gave a loud shout as I fought back against him. I grabbed his arms and put my foot flat against his stomach. For once, I could see he was scared and that was the last thing I see as I lifted him up with my foot and kicked out, launching him over my head and propelling him through the air. At the same time, I done a backward roll off the side of the walkway but managed to grab on to the walkway, feeling the strain of holding on nearly ripping my arm off. I screamed in pain. Just as I did, I heard a splash from beneath me and just had time to look down and see Henrich disappear in a vat of green liquid. I heard him screaming even as he went under and the liquid filled his lungs. Then there was silence. I still wasn't quite out if danger, I was still hanging precariously over the edge of the chemicals and my muscles were screaming at me to let go. But I held on and grabbed the edge with my other hand and with the last of my strength, hoisted myself back over to safety. I lay there resting for a moment going over the last few moments in my head.

My father.

He knew my father.

He practically said as much.

The only question was how?

Chapter 11

The Attack

It was a couple of days later. When I got home after my confrontation with Henrich. Ray, Paige and Faith were waiting for me. First looking annoyed at me being so late when we were meant to be scoping out the mansion and then concerned and had a look of disbelief on their faces. They all began asking questions at once. All of them along the lines of what the hell happened? So I told them all about the person asking for help down the alleyway, then the ensuing fight with Henrich. The other three just sat there listening, hardly believing the story. After they got over the shock, Faith helped me get cleaned up. Which I preferred to the time Ray fixed me up. She took me upstairs to the bathroom.

"Ouch" I yelped when she was taking care of the blow to my head.

"Oh don't be such a baby" she joked. "I'm really glad you didn't die".

"Yeah I'm sort of happy about that myself" I

said back with a smile. We both looked deep into each others eyes. Her beautiful hazel eyes. Her face came closer to mine as she continued cleaning my wound. I could smell the sweet scent of her perfume. She stopped dabbing at the wound and was just staring into my eyes. Her face was edging closer to mine, her lips slightly parted. I realised she was going for a kiss. I could feel butterflies erupting in my stomach. I was nervous but that didn't stop me responding. It was actually happening.

"How you doing mate?" Ray came into the doorway and interrupted the moment. I shot an evil glance towards him. But Faith was calm.

"He's all fixed up" she replied. "Just be more careful from now on" she said to me before leaving.

"Looks like she took real good care of you" Ray said with a smile before disappearing. I cursed him under my breath.

"Oh well, better luck next time" I whispered to myself.

*****

The next night we scouted the mansion like we wanted to the night before. We stayed quite a distance away looking through binoculars. We found a big warehouse that looked similar to where I fought Henrich. We made our way up the fire escape ladders which took us all the way to the roof. We all was making sure no one could see us but we were dressed in black and moving slowly so I was fairly certain no one could see us. We reached the roof in good time. It was a flat roof with raised edges. There was a couple of skylights which when we looked inside, told us the buildings were nothing special. Just some ordinary looking machinery which was used to make something. There was a fire exit door which would lead back inside but which also wouldn't be able to be opened from this side. We crouched down over the side facing up the street towards the mansion. We wanted to get a lay of the land. There was a long road that led towards the mansion so you could see any vehicles coming for miles. We was in the middle of an industrial estate with some factories around. From my vantage point I could see the factory where Henrich now laying in a vat of green liquid. Closer to the mansion we could see some nice houses where the more wealthy residents clearly lived. They all had their own land and had detached houses meaning some even had alleys in between them.

We then turned our attention to the mansion. We began by taking in the guards positions and the time they switched. It was a fairly obvious routine. Three different shifts. Faith and Paige already knew there was a guard switch at 2 pm. There was a morning shift from 6 am till 2 pm. The afternoon shift was 2 pm till 10 pm. And the night shift was 10 pm till 6 am. The night shift was when we would make our move so we could use nightfall as cover. There was a guard on the balcony overlooking the main road into the mansion who was armed with a sniper rifle. Then there was a few around the entrance to the mansion. We could see two permanently guarding the door whilst another couple was patrolling around the entrance. Possibly with more guards that we couldn't see. We always knew it wouldn't be easy but it was beginning to look more impossible by the minute. Ray sighed.

"I'm not liking our chances" Ray said. Inside I was agreeing. How could four normal people overcome a small army armed to their eyeballs.

"What other choice do we have?" Faith asked rhetorically. I knew she was right. We may have a slim chance but we couldn't stand by and do nothing.

"I know it's going to be hard but we never thought it was going to be easy. Something is going on here. There's something weird about this leader and he's keeping the old one hostage and torturing him. And I for one intend to try my hardest to find out why. Who's with me?" Faith asked whilst extending her hand out in the middle of us intending to make a pact. I extended my hand out and lay it on top of hers to show her I was with her. I felt her soft skin underneath mine. Once more I had butterflies erupt in my stomach. It happened every time we touched. I noticed her blush slightly and give me that beautiful smile. Next Paige followed and put hers on top of mine.

"Ah what the hell? I always like a challenge" Ray said before putting his hand on top of Paige's.

"So it's settled. We infiltrate tomorrow" Faith said.

*****

The next day was the same as any other. I got up, got ready and left. Nothing happened as nothing rarely happens. The day just went by like the breeze flowing through the air. It was coming to the end of the day. I was ready, already psyching myself up for tonight. It was 4 30 pm and everybody began winding down getting ready to leave. It seemed emptier today like there was a lot of guards that wasn't there but I didn't take much notice of it. I was looking back into town preparing to make my journey back to Paige's. I heard murmuring around me. Some of the guards talking excitedly. There were a few of them looking in the distance back over the wall. More of them started to rise up to get a better look and talking to each other hurriedly. I gazed out into the distance to see what the fuss was about. I could see something in the distance but I wasn't sure what it was. I picked up a pair of binoculars and looked into them. Immediately I felt sick. It was some wolves. But it wasn't just one or two. There was loads of them. Easily over 100. Possibly closer to 200. The likelihood is they wouldn't make it past the defences but we still got into defence positions.

They approached the minefield. I sat back knowing in a couple of seconds they would be getting blown up or running scared at the very least. They were still running at full speed so they would have no chance.

Nothing happened.

They had crossed over the start of the minefield and nothing happened. No explosions, no bangs, no deaths. They just carried on running, getting closer to us.

Why hadn't the mines worked?

It was a question that needed answering a different time as we prepared for the attack. The machine gun turrets would still be able to cut a lot of them down. They approached the turret range rapidly.

Again nothing happened. No machine gun turrets rising from the ground. The ground just lay still underneath the stampede of wolf feet. Now people were panicking. They had never had an attack of this size and now the defences wasn't even working. But surely with the size of this wall they wouldn't have anyway of infiltrating but we took no chances and readied our guns and weapons. Most loading up and taking aim, myself included. We waited until they got closer. They came into range.

Instantly guns started sounding all around. Some machine guns, some snipers and even a couple of handguns. I was firing a standard M240 Machine gun. A gun previously used in the US Army. It was the guns we were all supplied with. We took out a few before they even reached the wall. I was aiming down the scope and took two down in an instant, one after the other. They approached the wall still running at speed. This would be easy pickings as they wouldn't be able to scale the wall.

Then the impossible happened.

They began jumping at the wall, as they did, they extended their legs out and their vicious paws clawed at the wall and sunk deep into it. They had grown such powerful legs and paws that they were able to penetrate the bricks and mortar. The hybrids were stronger than ever. They began bounding up the wall. Around me a few of the guards began retreating like cowards abandoning their posts and not facing the beasts head on. The majority, however, were still there trying to defend the town. A lot of them were panicking, as was I, but we didn't show it. We remained defiant.

We had took out a lot of them already from when they were approaching the wall. But it wasn't enough. There was still at least 100 left. All clambering up the wall. When one wave moved, the next waved bounced onto the wall and began climbing up. The first wave just took a last jump to get on top of the wall. One jumped right for me. I brought my machine gun up just in time to let a cascade of bullets slam into his body then the beast lay lifeless. Another couple further down the wall had reached the top. They had just began mauling a couple of the guards. Their piercing screams going through the air. I swung my machine gun round and let off more bullets into them. Not before they had done the damage though. The guards lay there, one not moving at all. Dead. The other still screaming with massive chunks taken from his leg.

Another wave was on top of the wall and again I brought my machine back around to let off more bullets but this time I was too slow. A wolf caught the machine gun in his mouth and wrestled it from my hands before crushing it with its monstrous teeth. Now it was just me and the beast but I still had my Crusader sword with me so I unsheathed it and began swiping at the beast, narrowly missing it. It retaliated, snapping its jaw at me but I was too quick and dodged him and brought my sword round and buried it into the beast. It writhed in agony and then lay still. More wolves arrived at the top of the wall. We were still fending them off. Some guards still had their guns bombarding the wolves. Others had lost their guns and were using a variety of swords, knives and daggers to kill. Others were losing their battle and taking their last breath.

I did what I could to help others. I was swinging my sword around trying to kill all the wolves I could. But more of them just kept arriving over the top of the wall. Soon we would be overrun which made me realise something. Surely the new guards should have been here by now. The changeover is always at the same time and yet today there was no sign of anybody. I looked back over the town expecting to see the cavalry arriving. But I knew it was more hope than expectation. There was no one coming. We were on our own.

We still fought back. We were losing more than we were killing but that didn't stop us. A wolf came charging towards me, I quickly sidestepped and swung my sword slicing through its neck. Just as I did, another one reached the top of the wall but I put my sword through its head before it could do anything and then I watched it fall back 50 feet to the ground knocking a couple of other wolves off the wall with it. Another wolf had just finished its meal with a guard before it turned its attention to me. It was snarling showing its vicious set of fangs. It began charging at me. I noticed something in the corner of my eye. It was a sawed-off shotgun. It was leaning up against the wall. I grabbed it and swivelled on the spot just as the wolf sprang in the air to attack.

It didn't stand a chance. I brought the shotgun up and blasted it back to where it came. I felt the huge force erupt from the barrel. But I wasn't done there. Wolves seemed to come at me from all directions. With each one, they were met with the same fate. A shotgun blast. Another two dead. Three more. I was almost having fun. Then I heard the click indicating I had no ammo left. Another wolf was attacking. This time I brought the shotgun round and slammed the barrel into the face. But it wasn't enough. The wolf got back up and pounced on top of me. Its jaws were snapping at me inches from my face. I could smell its vile breath and see the saliva dripping from its mouth. I managed to retrieve my dagger and slammed it into the beast. It yelped and lay still. I threw it off of me and stood up, regaining my composure.

Now I was stood up, I wish I would have played dead. I had five wolves surrounding me. One by one I could do it but five at the same time. I had no chance. But if this was going to be my final moment, I would at least take a couple with me. I gripped my sword tighter and waited for them to make their move. They was circling and snarling preparing to attack. Just as they were about to make their move, someone came running up behind them and separated two of their heads from their body. This was my chance and I took it. I brought my sword through the air and through one of the beasts bodies and then brought it back out and down through another one, slicing it open. As I did another one attacked the guy that helped and he brought his sword up going through his throat and unceremoniously dumping it to the ground. It was only now I looked at the guy and realised who it was.

"Ray!" I exclaimed.

"Couldn't let you have all the fun could I?" He joked.

"But how did you know?" I asked.

"I heard one of the cowards who was meant to be defending us say and I came up as quick as I could. Oh and I brought some friends" Ray said. Right on cue, I heard lots of yelling as a load of guards climbed the wall and began decimating the wolves. One by one the wolves numbers gradually got less and less. Within a few minutes it was over. Any remaining wolves were dealt with swiftly and tossed over the side of the wall.

"I don't understand how they got here? What happened to the defences?" Ray asked.

"I don't know but I intend to find out" I replied. I pulled one of the guards aside to ask him some questions.

"Where were you lot? You were supposed to take over from us. If you got here on time, none of this would have happened" I said.

"We were told to come an hour later" he replied.

"By who?" I asked.

"By Max." Max was the head of the guards. He was in charge of what time the shifts were but any change, everybody would be notified. So why hadn't anyone known about the change and why did he change it.

"Apparently he also told a lot of the guys to take the day off" the guard said. So that's why there seemed like less guards because Max had told them to take the day off.

"Something's not right here. And I need to find out what" I said. Ray nodded his head and we both took off down the wall. There wasn't much conversation as we walked back to Paige's. We were both trying to figure out what was going on we scarcely realised we had come to Paige's house.

The door was already open. We walked inside and were met by a bombsite. There was papers all over the floor. A smashed window. A bookcase turned over. The sofa upside down. Ray and I both took out our swords.

"Faith. Paige." I called out.

"Up here" we were greeted by a weak voice that we recognised as Paige's. We both ran up the stairs. Paige was lying on the floor. She looked injured but otherwise unharmed.

"What happened?" I asked.

"Faith and I were just talking when there

was a knock. And a couple of seconds later the door swung open. There was a lot of the leaders personal guards that came in. We tried to fight them off but there was too many of them" she explained.

"What about Faith? Paige. Where's Faith?" I asked. Tears were in her eyes and I already knew the answer.

"They've taken her."

Chapter 12

The Infiltration

Faith was all I could think about. We spent all night deciding the best plan of attack. It was best not to attack that night when we wasn't thinking clearly as we would be at higher risk of capture or death. At least Ray and Paige were thinking it. I just wanted her back. I was awake all night, staring at the ceiling. Tossing and turning trying to recover some energy. Eventually morning came and I only managed a couple of hours sleep. More than I expected. I was still thinking about Faith. I just had to make it through today and then tonight, no one would stop me from rescuing Faith.

"Eat something mate. You're going to need your strength" Ray said pulling me out of my daze.

"I'm not hungry" I replied sternly. It may have seemed rude but Ray didn't say anything. He knew what was on my mind.

The day went by in a blur. I went from Paige's to the wall but I don't even remember the journey. I took my position and almost didn't move for the next eight hours just thinking about tonight. The wall had been cleared of all the bodies. All the men that had died would be given a proper burial whilst all the beasts were disposed of. As soon as I could leave, I did just that. I walked rapidly back to Paige's eager to get tonight underway. When I got back, Paige was already there but Ray hadn't come back yet.

"I thought I would make the two of you a good meal to keep your energy up" Paige said.

"Thanks" I said with a smile. After thinking about Faith all day, I had to admit I was more hungry than I thought and some food would do me good. Ray returned home and Paige served up the dinner. I wolfed down the food wanting to get out there as soon as possible.

"Easy mate. You'll give yourself indigestion" Ray said but I took no notice. The time was eight o'clock. Time to leave.

"Make sure you rescue Faith and come back in one piece" Paige said before giving me a massive hug. I smiled at her and stepped out the door.

"Listen. If anything happens tonight, I just want you to know…" Ray was cut off mid-sentence by Paige planting a kiss on his lips.

"You better come back" was all that Paige said.

"Yeah. You bet" Ray said in a slightly higher pitched tone than usual for once losing his cool. We left the house and made our way to the mansion. Neither of us said much on the way, we were both just concentrating on what was about to happen. We arrived at the same old abandoned warehouse where we was a couple of days ago when we were staking the place out. It had a good view of the mansion so we would know the most opportune moment to start executing our plan. We had just over an hour until the guards changed shift. We decided to wait for a couple of hours before beginning to infiltrate. An hour passed by quite quickly. We had some binoculars and every so often we would look to see if anything had changed but it was no surprise there was nothing. Mostly we just waited to see the changing of guards. Every so often one of us would try to strike up a conversation but it was no good. We was filled with a mix of emotions. Nervous at the thought of trying to break in. Scared at the thought one of us may not make it. Angry that they had Faith. Now we were just feeling impatient. The sooner we started, the sooner we wouldn't be feeling anything and we could just let the adrenaline take over.

Two large convoy trucks pulled up. I picked up the binoculars to get a closer look. The back opened up and it seemed like an endless stream of guards got out. This was obviously the night shift but it seemed like more guards than usual but then maybe the leader had been anticipating a retaliation. Ray whistled.

"That's a lot of people to get through" he said. I knew he was right. This was insane. This was suicide. But we had no choice.

"Listen Ray. This is going to be dangerous. If you don't want to…"

"Don't even think about it mate. We're in this together. I know the risks but that's not stopping me" Ray said and smiled. I smiled back then went back to the binoculars. By now the guards had finished piling out of the trucks and the guards who had finished their shift was piling back into them. The trucks left. Now we just had to wait for another couple of hours before we began to execute our plan.

The two hours seemed to drag on for a lot longer. So much so Ray was even half asleep. The town around us grew silent and the only life we could see was that of the guards. I shook Ray from his daze.

"You ready?" I asked.

"I was born ready" he said with a yawn. We set off from the roof and began climbing back down to ground level. We didn't have much of a plan for inside because we didn't know what to expect but we had a plan to get inside. There was two guards outside the entrance and a sniper on the balcony above just like before. We wasn't getting anywhere close to the entrance with the sniper positioned above it. But fortunately there was still the two guards who were walking around the perimeter so it was a case of knocking them out and stealing their uniforms. We was at ground level again. We timed it well the two guards were just passing each other preparing to go round again.

"You take the left side, I'll take the right" I whispered to Ray. Ray nodded and set off. I set off in the opposite direction, taking cover behind some nice houses where the richer people lived. We had to make sure we couldn't be seen by the sniper otherwise the mission would be over before it began. I found a small alleyway between two houses and a dumpster to hide behind. When the guard was in earshot I whistled to hopefully draw his attention.

It worked. I saw him draw his gaze over to the alleyway. But he carried on dismissing it so I whistled again, slightly louder. This time definitely worked. He began walking over cautiously. He had brought his machine gun round to his hands ready to fire at any moment. I didn't dare look out from behind the dumpster as he would cut me down as soon as I did. I could hear his footsteps getting closer in the dark. I had to use my ears more as my eyes were struggling down this alleyway in the dark. I waited and waited till he was close enough.

Then I pounced.

Appearing like a ninja in the dead of night. He saw me too late. His eyes widened in surprise and I knew he was about to bring his machine gun up but he didn't have a chance. I gave him a straight kick to the knee, hearing the bone snap. He crumpled to one knee and then I drove a swift elbow to his temple. His body lay on the floor, unconscious. It was everything I could do to not finish the job there and then. To kill him. I was so angry just because of who he worked for but I knew I had to be better than that. He was defenceless, I couldn't kill him in cold blood.

I wouldn't.

I tied him up and set him behind the dumpster. He would be out for a few hours. I then stripped him and changed my clothes. Within a couple of minutes I had transformed from a rebel trying to infiltrate the mansion to one of the leaders personal bodyguards. Dressed up in old style American army uniform. If only father could see me now, he'd be so proud.

I came out from the alleyway continuing on his patrol route, I just hoped Ray had also completed his side because if he hadn't it was game over already. I was returning to walk past the mansion. We just had to hope no one would recognise us but I kept my hat as low as possible hoping to cover my face. I saw the other guard that I had to pass, I just had to hope that it was Ray. We was getting closer to each other but I was too scared to look up in case something had gone wrong. Still we continued closer till our paths were about to cross. I chanced a look up. Thankfully I saw Ray's face winking back at me. Time to execute the next phase of our plan clearing the two in front of the entrance.

"Oi, you" one of the guards said. Crap, I thought. Myself and Ray both looked up wondering who they were speaking to. When I looked up, their eyes told me they were speaking to me. I gave a signal to Ray to indicate not to do anything yet so I could see what they wanted first. It could be nothing I thought. Ray continued slowly on his route not wanting to stray too far from the action. I began cautiously making my way towards them. As I approached I could see that both of them had blank faces with no distinguishing features as if they had been trained to look that way.

"What's up?" I tried asking casually.

"You got any cigarettes? I'm dying for a smoke" one of the guards asked. I breathed a sigh of relief whilst also seeing my opportunity.

"No, but I think that guy over there might" I said nodding in the direction of Ray.

"Hey, guy" I shouted over to Ray. He was still close enough to hear. He turned his head.

"You got any smokes?" I shouted to him again. I just hoped he would see what was going on. At first he looked slightly puzzled but then realised what I was trying to do.

"Yeah sure" Ray tried his best not to sound too Australian. He walked over to us, pretending to check his pockets. He just reached us when he went into his trouser pocket, pretending to bring some cigarettes out but instead of a cigarette packet he brought his fist flying out and connecting with the side of the guards jaw who then fell to the floor knocked out. As he did this, I grabbed the other guard from behind and put him in a sleeper hold which eventually knocked him out also. Now we knew it was only a matter of time before the sniper realised what was going on and would sound the alarm.

Ray and myself worked fast. We opened the door to the mansion, being careful to make sure there were no guards waiting for us behind the door. Luckily there wasn't. We remembered certain parts from our time here before but we only saw a limited amount on the previous visits so the majority of this place would still be new to us. We saw where we had to go though. There was a grand, clean, white staircase in front of us. The type you'd expect in a mansion. Above us was a balcony running around the room with it leading back to the balcony we saw outside. On the ground either side of the stairs was doors leading to different parts of the mansion. I guessed it probably meant east wing and west wing. We went east wing both times before but that wasn't our priority right now. That was getting to that sniper before it was too late.

"Come on. You can admire the place later" Ray said in a hurried whisper. He was right. We had to move fast. I ran up the stairs with Ray just behind me. I turned the corner and changed my run to a hurried walk so I wouldn't alert anybody nearby. Ray was just getting to the top of the stairs.

"Hey, what are you doing?" A guard had appeared through a door at

the top of the stairs. He was speaking to Ray and hadn't seen me yet. It was lucky we was wearing the same uniforms otherwise Ray would have been dead already. Ray had stopped in his tracks facing the guard.

"I said, what are you doing?" he asked again.

"I don't suppose you'd believe me if I said looking for the toilet" Ray joked not trying to hide his accent but it didn't matter by that time I was directly behind and before he could react. I put my hands around his neck and twisting it sharply, I heard the neck snap before he lied in a heap on the floor.

"Take care of the other one, I'll hide this one" I said urgently to Ray. I knew the only feasible place to hide his body would be back in the room where he came from. I checked inside to see if anymore guards were inside. The coast was clear. It turned out to be an armoury with all manner of weapons inside. Ranging from pistols to shotguns. Sniper rifles even to an RPG. I hid the body and went back to the door to check if anymore guards had appeared. There were none. As I came back out I heard a scuffle and then I saw Ray dragging a body in from the balcony. The sniper. He also hid the body in the armoury.

"So far, so good" Ray said. I thought the same thing but didn't want to jinx it. We made our way back down the stairs. We had the choice of either east or west. We went east, knowing the best place to go would be the dungeons where we saw Marcus being tortured. We went through the door, knowing we had to take care with each step, expecting to encounter a plethora of guards. I took the lead and made sure the coast was clear, sneaking down a hallway, doors were on either side of us and I was expecting one of them to crash open at any second but it never came. Ray then proceeded to take the lead and took the same care while I watched our backs but there was nothing. It was silent. Either we were getting extremely lucky or something was up. But we had no other choice but to carry on. To rescue Faith. We turned the corner at the end of the hallway and still no one was there.

At the end was the dining room and if you turned left, it led to the massive ballroom we were in before. But we knew we had to get to the dining room and get back to the dungeons. We came to the end of the next hallway. I could see the dining room just in front as I was about to walk out, a guard came out from around the corner. He was shocked to see us and we were almost shocked since we didn't encounter any guards on the way. His gun was on his hip and he didn't have time to reach for it so instead he went with his fist which I was quick to dodge before turning and driving my elbow into the side of his head knocking him unconscious.

"Well looks like not everybody's asleep" Ray said. I nodded.

"Let's go" I replied. We went into the dining room. It was unchanged from the last time we were there. The same table with everything exactly in the same place. The same painting on the wall which I knew housed a TV behind it where the leader spoke to us a couple of days before. And the same fireplace which I knew housed the secret entrance to the dungeons. I went straight over to the fireplace.

"This is it" I said to Ray who had never seen the secret entrance before. I pulled the candelabra as Faith had the other day.

Nothing happened.

I tried again, this time pulling harder. Still

nothing happened.

"Are you sure that's right?" Ray questioned.

"Yeah this is definitely what Faith done" I replied. I gave it one last yank and almost broke it but still the fireplace stayed as it was. Something was wrong. This was only working the other day but now nothing.

Suddenly all the doors slammed shut around us and locked shut. Every single one of them was open and now there was no way out. We were supposed to be rescuing Faith from a prison and now we were imprisoned ourselves. I looked at Ray and he looked at me and we had both came to the same realisation.

It was a trap.

Chapter 13

The Rescue

Immediately I went to the nearest door set next to the fireplace and tried opening it but it wouldn't budge. Ray done the same to another door with no luck.

"We're trapped" Ray said with panic rising in his voice. I was about to try and calm him down when a mechanical whirring started. The same noise we heard a couple of days before. The painting. It was beginning to slide in two as it had before to reveal the TV behind it. The other day it showed the leader. I wondered if it would be the same this time.

The TV was now fully revealed and the screen flickered on. Sure enough it was the same as before. The silhouette of the leader showing on the screen.

"Welcome again. This is now the third time you have decided to enter my premises" he said. So he knew we were here at the ball. It's like everything that happened has been because he wanted it to happen.

"I had to take precautions to not allow you back into the dungeon but if you wanted to have a look down there again. You only had to ask" the leader continued. The TV changed from the silhouette of the leader to a dark, dreary place I recognised as the dungeons. But there was no sign of the previous person who occupied it. Instead there was a beautiful woman sat in a lone metal chair. Her face was bruised and swollen like she had been in a thousand fights and had something in her mouth clearly to stop her from talking or screaming. Her face was wet from tears that had been cried. Her hands and feet were also tied up.

It was Faith.

But she wasn't alone. There was a guard standing next to her with a pistol. The pistol was pointing at her head.

"Faith." It came out as a whisper. The TV flickered back to the leader.

"You have my word that no more harm will come to her as long as you follow my simple instructions. Number 1: Throw your guns and swords and any other weapons you may be hiding towards the door nearest to you" the leader demanded. After a moments pause, we knew there wasn't anything we could do. We done as he instructed and within seconds the door swung open and some guards came in and took the weapons and disappeared.

"The next instruction is fairly simple. You die." At that moment all the doors swung open and guards poured into the room from every door. All carrying swords and daggers of a different variety. We were unarmed. We were helpless.

"I guess all that's left to say is goodbye. But don't worry about Faith. I'm sure she'll be very comfortable in her new home" the leader continued. Once again the TV flickered to the dungeon showing Faith being held hostage. Then it clicked off and the painting began closing.

The guards all began converging on us. Ray and myself backed towards the fireplace, standing side by side so at least we could see all of them. But it wouldn't do no good without anything to defend ourselves with.

They continued to close in. All of them clearly well trained in the art of swordplay.

"There's too many of them, we don't stand a chance" Ray said.

"We have no choice" I replied. And with that, something burned inside of me. Adrenaline began pumping its way through my body. All of a sudden I wasn't scared. I was pumped. I was almost excited. I was delirious. I let out a yell and ran head first into the nearest of my attackers. They were clearly caught off guard thinking I would beg for my life. But that wasn't me.

I ran up to the first two guards and without a moments hesitation, aimed my fist at the guard to the right. Both guards were so startled, they didn't have time to react with the swords only slightly lifting them up. My fist connected with the mans stomach, knocking all of the wind out if him. As soon as I had done it, I brought my foot round connecting a roundhouse kick to the second guards jaw, leaving them both crumpled on the floor. I picked up one of the swords. Not quite as special as my one but it would do. It was a standard backsword. I continued running towards the next wave. I swung my sword through the air as did the opposing guard, hearing the audible clink as the two swords connected but I reacted quicker with the second blow, raising my sword and bringing it cutting through the air and slicing down his body. He let out a roar of pain and then laid still on the floor. Dead. Blood pouring from his body.

I had no time to look though as another came for me from the side. I sidestepped his lunge pivoting on my left foot and facing away from the guard while I brought my sword and plunged it through his stomach and quickly pulled it out again so it wouldn't get stuck. I was facing the opposite direction to the rest of the guards for a second and noticed Ray slaughtering the guards on the other side. He was holding a mace with a few bodies lying on the floor around him.

I turned back to the oncoming guards. Another two guards were charging at me in perfect harmony but I already had a plan. I slid down between them, none of them reacting quick enough. I pounced back to my feet, swinging my sword through the air killing one of them before having to sidestep the next guard. I swung my sword up, severing the arm that was holding his weapon from his body. He let out a cry of anguish before I put him out of his misery by severing his head from his body. Every part of him lay still, blood cascading from everywhere.

By now, a lot of the floor had turned red. The blood of my enemies becoming a stream underneath my feet. But they still seemed to be coming. It was never ending. I turned back to Ray who was still battling with everything he could muster. Sweat dripping down his face. For a moment, we shared a glance and I could tell we both had that same look in our eye. Defeat.

Another guard had just reached me and I quickly brought my sword back up to defend myself but I was hit with such force that it sent me stumbling back. The guard took his chance and brought his sword back slicing down the back of my leg. This time I let out a roar of pain as I was sent down to one knee. I knew the death blow was coming. I raised my sword in defiance. Determined not to be beaten. Faith was counting on me. I had a new surge of adrenaline. My sword protected me from the fatal blow and I quickly used my position to my advantage. From one knee I plunged my sword through his stomach and then retracted it again. I was ready for the next wave when Ray's voice sounded over the fighting.

"Blake, it's no good. We can't keep going like this" he was shouting in between not being killed. But I knew he was right, we needed to do something otherwise we wouldn't last too much longer.

"Go" he continued shouting. "I'll hold them off, you need to get to Faith. Go now!" I would have argued but he was right. This was pointless. We wasn't going to win this fight and Faith is the reason we're here. I was on my feet and began charging towards the door. I was going for the same door we came in through as I knew my way in this area and didn't want to get lost searching for Faith. There was still plenty of guards to fight through before the door but they didn't stand a chance. The first one swung his blade through the air but I had already ducked and was swinging my blade towards him ending his life in an instant. The next one plunged his sword towards me but again I was too quick, sidestepping before slicing through him. I was in the clear going through the door.

SLAM!!!

It felt like I had been hit by a brick wall. I

was sent tumbling to the floor. My sword was sent flying from my hand and skidded along the floor out of reach. I was dazed and confused lying on the floor. Suddenly I was hoisted off the ground and was hanging with my feet a few inches off the ground. I was now face to face with the biggest person I had seen yet. He was enormous and was lifting me about like I was a doll. He had a sick smile on his face because he had me where he wanted me. Or so he thought.

I brought both of my hands up and brought them crashing down into either side of his neck. Stunned, he let me go. I landed on my feet and sent a driving fist to his stomach but it didn't have any effect through his layers of muscle and fat. He had recovered from the strike to his neck and with surprising speed and agility, threw his right hand in my direction wrapping his knuckles against the side of my face, sending me hurtling across the hallway and skidding across the floor. The left side of my face felt like it was on fire, pain searing through my cheek. I touched my cheek feeling how tender and bruised it was. I spat which came out pure red. Blood.

I had to find a way to defeat this gargantuan of a human. And quick. But not before he came rushing at me, grabbed me and threw me back to where I came from. Once again, crashing to the floor feeling my whole body rock. I looked around me for anything I could use. There. Set in the side of the wall. I noticed a fire extinguisher. The guard had just began his next attack, coming at me with ferocity but I was ready. I swung the extinguisher round as hard as I could, connecting with the mans head. He stumbled back, I thought for sure he would be knocked out but instead he came back angrier. So instead I put it to its second use. I pulled the pin and aimed the hose in his direction. Then I squeezed the trigger and foam erupted from the end. I sprayed it in his face until there was no more left. But still he swung a right hand which connected underneath my chin and once again sent me flying. He was squealing in pain whilst trying to rub his eyes to see. I was on the floor feeling like I couldn't go on till I noticed a glistening at the corner of my eye. I began crawling over to the object, but not before I heard the stomping of the guards feet. He had clearly recovered enough to come and finish me off. But it was too late. I had reached the glistening object which was the sword I had dropped before. I picked it up and swung it back in the guards direction. There was hardly a sound as my sword met his flesh and continued straight through. That was until his head rolled off from his body and hit the ground with a thump.

I slumped to the ground, bruised, bloody and beaten. But I couldn't stop. I hadn't defeated that monstrous man just to give up. Slowly, I made my back to my feet and continued. I half ran, half limped back to the entrance. Only now remembering my previous injury on my leg. I encountered no guards but then I wasn't surprised. I thought all the guards must have been sent to deal with us and there probably wouldn't be too many other guards about. I went the west wing side this time. Having never been here before I took my time. Clearly people wasn't meant to see this side. Whereas the east side was filled with grand paintings and pristine floors. The west side was bare and empty. There was a long hallway with multiple doors set on each side. I thought the best bet for dungeons would be downstairs. Sure enough, down the end I could see steps leading down. I quickly raced to the stairs, still not encountering another person. I took a few steps down and became shrouded in darkness. Only a few lit candles lighting the way ahead. Once again this was different. It was dingy and damp down here but I was sure this was the right place.

I continued my descent, feeling the coldness that comes with the dungeon sweeping over me. The sound of my feet tapping against the steps was the only sound other than the sound of my thumping heart. But then I heard voices. They travelled effortlessly though the air with no other sounds to interrupt them.

"Your friends have no chance, they're most likely already dead" I heard a voice taunting someone. He had a strange foreign accent.

"I still believe. They have the biggest hearts of anyone I've ever met" I recognised the second voice as Faith's. I could tell she was fighting back the tears and trying to be strong. But so could the guard.

"If you want to cry. That's fine but it will probably be the last thing you do" the guard said. I could hear the sneer on his face as he said it.

"I wouldn't give you the satisfaction" Faith replied. At that comment, I smiled. She wasn't going to give up easily. I began moving down the last few steps. I got to the bottom and was greeted by a single corridor. It was still dimly lit by a few candles. At the bottom of the steps was the single wooden desk with a chair behind it that I saw before but from the other end. There was still no guard there. And down the end was the sweeping staircase I knew would take me to the secret fireplace where Ray was fighting. I hoped.

On the right was a row of five cells, each with the door open. I remember Marcus being tortured here and it made me wonder. How many loved ones had disappeared in this small town?

I crept even more quietly now I was getting closer. The voices seemed to be coming from the end cell. As I walked past each cell, I glanced inside. Each one seemed to be the same. They contained the same thing. A single iron bed, one bare lightbulb hanging from the ceiling and a filthy toilet in the corner. There was also a single camera fixed to the corner of the ceiling so that the demonic leader could keep an eye on his victims. There was nothing more, no windows. I could only imagine the sort of torture people must have endured in this place. I came to the fourth cell but this one looked a bit different. The bed had been flipped upside down, the mattress was heaped into the corner and toilet had a chunk missing as if someone's head had been thrown into it. Then I remembered. This was the cell Marcus had been getting tortured in. Clearly a fight had broken out and I was sure that Marcus hadn't won.

"Looks like no one is coming" the guard said from the next room which whipped me back to what I was supposed to be doing. I was just outside the last cell door when I heard the audible click of a gun being prepared to fire. I turned the corner. The guards back was facing towards the door with his pistol aimed at Faith's head. Her eyes were still glistening from the tears she had cried. Upon seeing me, her eyes widened with surprise. I lunged forward to attack the guard before he could pull the trigger but at the last second he sidestepped so quickly it caught me off guard and I had to stop myself from hitting Faith. I just had a second to look at Faith before all the wind was knocked out of me and I was sent skidding along the floor and sent flying into the wall. Luckily, I kept hold of my sword during the impact and it was by my side. His fist had connected with my ribs. The impact of his punch felt like he had broken them. Now I was winded and dazed after hitting the wall.

How did he know I was there? Had he heard me? As if he heard my questions he answered.

"Her eyes gave you away. And now I have the pleasure of killing you while she watches" now I had a chance to look at him, he had short, messy hair cut and an unshaven face. He had deep blue eyes and stained teeth. He was the wearing the same uniform as everyone else in the leaders army and his hand was holding a gun and it was pointed at me. He smiled and I saw his finger tighten around the trigger. There was nothing I could do.

BANG!!!

I heard the gunshot and everything seemed like it was in slow motion. Just before the gunshot, Faith had put all her energy into barrelling into the guard whilst still tied up. She crashed head first into the floor but she had done enough to put the guard off. He still got his shot away but it flew above my head and cannoned into the wall behind me. The guard stumbled but regained his composure and this time turned the gun on Faith. Now it was my turn. I pounced to my feet, picking my sword up just before I did and leapt across the room. The guard saw me coming and tried to turn his gun on me. But he was too late. I brought my sword down plunging through his chest and out the other side, as I did so, blood erupted from his mouth. He was skewered on my sword. He writhed over the sword and then lay still. I pulled my sword back out and his body hit the ground with a thump. I then wiped the blood off of my sword and went over to Faith.

"Faith! Are you okay?" I asked. I cut her restraints with my sword and helped her up. She was in a bad way. She needed medical attention. Her face was already bruised from the beating the guard must have given her and now there was a cut on the side of her head from her fall and blood was still seeping out of it. Her face was dirty and wet from the tears. I felt like she would fall over without me to help her stay on her feet. And yet a smile came across her face.

"I am now" she replied. Her face edge closer to mine. Even looking like that she was the most beautiful thing I had ever seen. Her lips parted slightly as I edged closer to her face.

BOOOOOOOM!!!

The loudest explosion I had ever heard erupted from upstairs. The whole room shook, bits of debris came flying off the wall, lightbulbs smashed and showered the rooms with glass. A toilet was knocked out of the wall and water cascaded from the hole that was now left.

"Ray" I shouted. I immediately headed for the stairs we used before in the hope that I could get through the fireplace this way. I heard Faith behind me as I bounded up the stairs taking them two or three steps at a time. I reached the top and thankfully the secret entrance opened up.

Immediately I felt searing heat and then I stepped through and realised why.

The whole place was an inferno. There were bodies everywhere. But there was no sign of Ray. Faith and I made our way through the flames, coughing and sputtering. Everything was ablaze, the great, ornate table. The majestic paintings. The gargantuan walls. Nothing escaped the fires wrath. And it was still spreading, going through walls. Then we saw him. On the other side of the room. Not moving. Ray!

We both darted over to him when suddenly a guard appeared from nowhere, attempting to cut me down. But I was too quick for him and dodged back before slicing through his stomach. Clearly not everyone was dead. I just hoped Ray wasn't. I crouched to his side.

"Ray! Ray!!" I yelled at him. Willing him to wake up. I heard him groan. I breathed a huge sigh of relief. But we couldn't celebrate yet. We still had flames dancing around us and we had to move before it was too late.

"Come on lets go" I shouted. I helped him to his feet and let him lean on my shoulder to keep himself up.

"Are you okay?" I asked to Faith.

"Yeah I'm fine, I can walk" Faith shouted over the destruction that was happening around us.

"What happened?" I asked to Ray.

"I told you I was saving that grenade for a rainy day" he said with a smile. I couldn't help but smile as well. The explosion must have set things on fire and from then it just spread. Even now as we half ran, half limped along to the exit. The flames leapt at us from its origin. The oxygen in the air giving it life. We went as fast as we could with Ray struggling to keep his feet and Faith still dazed but we made it to the exit. I smashed through the door and into the cool air. There was still no one around but I knew it wouldn't take long for the streets to fill up. Ray and Faith continued. Ray now able to walk more freely but I just stood at the door. Ray turned around to face me.

"What are you doing mate? The whole place is going to come down soon. We need to get away from here" Ray said.

"I can't" I replied. Ray and Faith just looked at me in disbelief.

"What do you mean you can't? Just put one step in front of the other" Ray said.

"I can't until I know for sure the leader is dead. Who's to say he won't survive and come back even worse. I can't rest until I know for sure that he is dead" I said. For a minute there was silence. The flames crackling up behind me.

"He's right" it was Faith who had spoke. She

was looking down at the ground.

"Who's to say he won't come back and be worse. The whole town will fall." She looked back up to me and I could see tears were falling from her eyes again. Her beautiful hazel eyes. She walked back to where I stood.

"But promise me. Promise me you'll kill him. And…" She hesitated.

"Promise me you'll come back?" She asked.

"I promise." No sooner had the words left my mouth before she launched herself at me and planted her lips on mine. I kissed her back and let our lips become one. Butterflies erupted in my stomach. She smiled and turned back making her way towards town. I turned to Ray who had a smile across his face.

"I'm not kissing ya" he jested before turning serious. "But come back safe. I've not known ya long but you're the best friend a guy could ask for" he said before extending his hand, which I shook. He then pulled me in for an embrace. He then also limped back towards Faith and towards town. I let the sight of them walking away towards town, towards safety engrave itself in my mind and allowed a small smile to come across my face. But now it was down to business. I would have to do this quick if I was to stand any chance of surviving. I turned around and darted back inside the mansion, running as fast as my feet would carry me. I knew going back east would be impossible as the fire was spreading rapidly and I hadn't seen any signs that the leader would be that way and the east wing looked like it just contained dungeons and a few other uninteresting places. So my best bet was the stairs in front of me. I leapt up the grand staircase and saw the door which lead to the armoury where we hid the bodies before. But next to it was another door I took no notice of before so I charged through that one. I was greeted by a long corridor with lamps at intervals illuminating the corridor. A red carpet was rolled the middle of the floor with tiling on either side of it. It reminded of the sort you would have for someone important. I felt like I was on the right tracks.

I sprinted down the corridor and slammed into the door. It was locked. I wasn't about to let a lock stop me. I slammed into the door using my shoulder as a battering ram. It didn't budge. But I wasn't giving up. I tried a couple more times unsuccessfully before I threw all of my weight behind it and smashed through to the other side sending the lock flying.

On the other side was a large room which looked similar to the living room me and my father used to have. There was a massive TV set on the wall and a luxury sofa in front of it. There was a massive oak table with chairs around it. There was different types of gaming machines scattered around the room. Ancient by the looks of them but clearly working. There was a huge bookcase along the back wall with a door set in the middle of it. To my right there was door so I went to it and opened it. But there was no one there, it was just a massive bathroom complete with luxury toilet and shower. I sprinted to the other side and opened a door but this just led to a massive stainless steel kitchen. It was so pristine, it looked like nothing was ever cooked in there. That just left the door in between the bookcases. Someone had to be behind this. I ran over to it and turned the door knob. The door swung open. There was a sofa to the right as I walked in with a lamp overlooking it. Further on from the sofa was another door. Dotted around the room was what looked like filing cabinets. Above the room was a chandelier glistening. A massive bear rug occupied the centre of the floor on an otherwise cream carpet. Around the room yet more magnificent paintings of different shapes, sizes and colours adorned the walls. In front of me was a huge desk, with a computer and a bank of telephones on it. Beyond the desk was a breathtaking window from wall to wall and floor to ceiling that looked out upon the horizon, facing away from the town. And in front of it there was a person. He had his back to me and was just a silhouette. Finally I had confronted the leader. It all came down to this.

"Finally. You can't hide anymore. I think its about time you showed your face" I said to him. He turned around and my heart stopped. It was impossible. I had to be dreaming. There's no way this could be real.

"Dad."

Chapter 14

Reunion

No. This couldn't be real. I saw him being mauled by a pack of wolves.

"What? How? Why?" The thousands of questions swirling around my head but none of them coming out. Through all this my father just stared at me, showing no emotion.

"I'm sorry son. I never wanted you to find out" was all he said. A gear inside me switched.

"What do you mean you never wanted me to find out?" I shouted and realised I was crying at the same time. This person. This man who was all I knew for most of my life and all he could say was 'I never wanted you to find out'. I was fuming.

"How could you do this to me? I'm your son!" I couldn't contain my anger.

"Would you let me explain?" He asked.

"How can you possibly explain this?" I retorted.

"It all started with the death of your mother" he started to explain. Again rage boiled inside me. My face must have showed this as he held his hand up to stop me interrupting.

"Please let me finish. When your mother died. It left a hole in me. You were born and I thought everything would be alright. I thought the hole would be filled. But it wasn't. No matter how hard I tried, all you did was remind me of her. I spent many nights, when you couldn't see me, crying and just wanting her back. But you can't raise the dead. And so I came up with a plan to try and forget about everything and spare me from any more pain. And that meant getting away from you."

I didn't know what to say. I was speechless. I was listening to what he was saying but the words seemed to make no sense to me. This man looked like my father. He sounded like my father. But it was like a completely different person.

"So I set a plan in motion. I spent years thinking of a plan and more years concocting it. I was going to train you well enough to survive. Through my experience in the army, I knew how to survive. Whilst I was training you, I spent my spare time thinking of a way to escape and the only real way I could think of was to fake my own death. So once I knew what to do, I just had to figure out how. One day whilst training you, I thought back to my days in the army. There was always top secret stuff that went on behind closed doors that the public never knew about. One of these things was mind control." I almost burst out laughing, he couldn't be serious.

"Mind control?" I questioned.

"Yes that's right. You may think its ridiculous but there were so many secrets in governments all over the world. It wouldn't surprise me if they are the reasons for this world we live in now. Anyway, I happened to be close to the head scientist working on this mind control. A brilliant scientist called Jonas Ulreich. He was born in Sweden but came to America as a child and was brought up as an American. I was always interested in this sort of thing and I picked up a thing or two from him. Of course since the end of the world, I hadn't thought about it. But then I remembered it and I began planning, designing, scavenging for things that would help create my device. It took many years but I finally made it." As he finished his sentenced, he pointed to something on his desk. I hadn't noticed it until now but there was a small grey device on the desk. It looked completely out of place in this world. This world that got sent back many years in the past through war and yet there was this small device that looked like it was sent from a thousand years in the future.

"Rather than just show it to you, why don't I show you what it can do" he said. It was only as he was picking it up and placing it around his ear, I realised what he meant but it was too late. Now I could see the device working, it was easier to see how it was designed. There was one wire with a tab on the end that stuck to the base of his neck that joined to the spine and a little red light which must have housed a micro sensor in it. This snaked around the ear and was connected to three more wires with tabs on the end and three more red lights on them. These tabs stuck to the side of his head and temple. Now he had put the device on, the red lights lit up, showing that it was working.

"Here!" He shouted and with that, the biggest, most demonic looking wolf I had ever seen walked through the door. It was snarling with saliva dripping from its mouth. Where all of the chunks of fur were missing you could see scars adorning the body.

"What are you doing?" I asked but I already knew the answer.

"I just wanted to give you a demonstration. Attack!" He said and with that the wolf lunged for me. I dived to the right to avoid the attack, barely doing so but it turned straight back round and was on me again straight away. Again I dived to my left this time and heard the snap of its jaws inches away from my neck. This time I decided to go on the offensive, launching myself in its direction, unsheathing my sword and going for the jugular. But it was too quick. It snapped its head in my direction and caught my sword between its teeth. I was now eye to eye with it and I could see the venom there as he crunched down with its teeth completely bending my sword and putting it out of action. The sword fell uselessly to the ground.

"What are you going to do now?" I heard my father say humorously. But he was right, I no longer had any weapons to defeat this beast. After everything I had done, this could be the end.

No. I had to believe I could beat it and wipe the smile off of my fathers face. I just needed a plan, I was searching around the room looking for anything I could use. A plan formulated in my mind. I just had to execute it. The beast was circling, readying its next attack. Without a moments notice, it flew straight for me, again I was too quick and darted round him but this time I ran straight towards the desk. My father was by the door the beast had come from watching curiously. I used the desk as a springboard, jumping over it to the other side, turning to face the beast once more. The gigantic window was behind me. As anticipated the wolf didn't hesitate in gunning for me again. It leaped up to the desk.

"No! Stop!" I heard my father yell but it was too late. Carried by momentum it had already leapt at me but I was no longer there. I had ducked down as the beast leapt straight over me and went crashing through the window and down the other side. I knew we were a few stories up so there was no way it would survive and sure enough I looked out of the window and it was laying there lifelessly.

A pool of blood began spreading from underneath its body. My father chuckled humourlessly.

"I see I taught you well" he said.

"How did you control that thing?" I asked panting.

"Anything with a brain can be controlled. You see I came up with the idea of controlling the wolves to attack me, apparently leaving me for dead."

"But the blood, all your wounds?"

"Yes I had to take a few hits to make it convincing" he lifted up his shirt as he spoke. He wasn't lying about taking a few hits, his whole body was covered in scars of varying shapes and sizes, all of different colours.

"They still hurt to this day but I had to suffer to get to my utopia. After this I began recruiting and building my army. Anybody with any military experience or any sort of muscle came with me. Some willingly, others not so" as he said it, he pointed to the device around his head.

"How did you know that there was anybody else? You always told me you had never seen anybody else" I asked.

"Do you remember that radio I used to have? The one that no one ever responded on?"

He asked. My face must have changed from confusion to recognition. Another thing he lied about.

"So I used the radio to contact other places and other people and began my network from there. Then I overtook this place and became the leader it deserves."

"You're nothing but a tyrant" I blurted out. As I said it, his face immediately changed and I could see anger coursing through him. He casually strolled over to me and without another word, belted me across the face with the back of his hand. The force of the impact sent me flying back and tumbling to the floor. I ended up near the shattered window. Searing pain coursed through my cheek as it turned bright red.

"That wasn't the only time I controlled them either. Remember the attack?" He asked. Of course, everybody said how unusual it was. Beasts never attack fortified towns and cities. That's what I was told and my father was obviously the reason for it. He told them to attack. He knew I understood.

"So you were responsible for everything? Deactivating the defences? The late changing of the guards? Henrich?" I asked struggling to look at him knowing he had done everything he could to kill me.

"Yes that's right. I was hoping they would

take you down then but you have proven quite resourceful but I won't make the same mistake again. Prepare to meet your end the same way my friend did." He gestured out of the window.

BOOM!!!

Another explosion even louder than any before shook the whole room. My father stumbled back. I knew I had to get the mind control device off of him otherwise I wouldn't stand a chance. I launched myself at him, using my shoulder as a battering ram into his stomach. I sent us both flying into the next room which turned out to be his bedroom. A lone bed laid in the corner with not much else around apart from a lightbulb hanging from the ceiling. I had him on the floor and unleashed my fist towards his head and connected. The device came flying off of his head. I expected him to be dazed but he struck back immediately letting his own punch fly. He connected with the other side of my face and sent me flying back through the door eventually backing into the desk. He came charging at me with lightning speed and sent his right fist driving into my stomach, immediately winding me before following it up with an uppercut. The force of his left hand connecting with my chin took me off my feet and I slammed into the desk knocking most of the items off. It was clear my father hadn't lost his speed or power in the years since he'd been gone.

I rolled off the side of the desk landing on all fours surrounded by the shattered glass. I spat and the saliva was pure red from biting my tongue due to the uppercut.

"I may have taught you everything you know but I didn't teach you everything I know. You still have a few things to learn" he said from behind. I heard the smile as he spoke. But I had a few tricks up my sleeve. I lashed out with my right foot connecting with his right shin but the force made him buckle over and his face slammed into the desk. I was slowly scrambling to my feet while he got up straight away. His nose had been busted from the impact and blood was streaming from it. His smile had disappeared and now his face was full of venom.

"That was dirty. I thought I taught you better than to fight dirty" he said.

"Looks like you didn't teach me everything" I replied. This time it was my turn to smile. He wiped the back of his hand over his face, smearing the blood. We both went charging at each other and it turned into an all out brawl. We exchanged punches back and forth both leaving the other battered and bruised. We both paused to catch our breath. Both of us breathing heavy. I looked at him, his whole face seemed swollen. His right eye looked like it would be sporting a bruise to match the busted nose and cut on his cheek. I knew I wasn't in any better condition though. I spat out a fresh batch of blood which served as a reminder that I was as bad as him.

"Looks like we're even" I said.

"We'll never be even. I am your father. I will always be too powerful for you" he replied trying to convince himself more than me.

The door suddenly slammed open almost coming off the hinges. We both snapped our head towards the door. Flames leapt up through the doorway. Through all the battle I had forgotten about the fire but now it seemed it had caught up. Intense heat came from the flames.

"Not only will you not die but now you've destroyed my home" he shouted. On the last word he came charging at me once again and let a right hook fly towards me. I brought my arms up to block it but the force of it still made me stumble and he took this opportunity to unleash his left hand towards my stomach, winding me and sending me to the floor. I could barely breathe. It was taking all my energy to try and force some air back into my lungs. I didn't even notice him walk over to me. It seemed like it took no effort for him to hoist me off the floor then launch me across the room towards the gaping hole where there used to be a window. I landed on the floor and then continued rolling along it, across all of the shattered glass. I felt a thousand stabbings at the same time, all tiny bits of glass piercing my skin and staying there. I ended up by the window, trying to get back to my feet but once again my father was on me before I had the chance.

He gave me a swift kick to my ribs to keep me down. I now realised I was hanging half out of the window. My body was still inside but my head was outside. Then my father pinned me down with his body and put his hands around my neck. He began squeezing and immediately I was struggling to breathe. He squeezed tighter and I began choking. My body screaming for some oxygen but not being given any. I tried to reach out for him with my hands but I ended up grabbing air. I had no energy to fight back. I could feel my life force being squeezed out of me. Black spots danced around my eyes. Soon I will black out and then I'd be helpless. All of a sudden images of people I loved, people I made promises to came to me. Ray, Paige and Faith. All of them swirling about in my head. It gave me one final bit of strength. One final push. I made them promises and I wasn't going to let them down.

I felt my right hand curl up into a fist then with the last of my energy, I unleashed towards where I hope my fathers head was. I felt his grip loosen, finally I could breathe. He was still on top of me and I was still hanging out of the window so I knew I had to continue on the offensive. I brought my head up from outside of the window and let the momentum carry on, connecting with my fathers head. He was sent tumbling back into the desk behind. I saw blood spreading from a deep gash on my fathers head, he was busted open bad but I couldn't stop. I got up to my feet, still getting my breath back. I ran up and clotheslined him over the desk. The fire was still blazing. The floor was disappearing beneath us. I hadn't noticed but there was no way out now. The whole doorway was ablaze and there would be no way through there but I couldn't think about my way out yet when I still had my father to deal with. He got up from the other side. His face was now all nearly covered in blood but his eyes showed so much anger, so much hatred. He let out a scream of anguish and overturned the desk but I quickly rolled to the left to avoid it. But he was on me almost before I could recover. He let out punch after punch. Left then right. I was struggling to keep up with his speed only just managing to block all of them but I could also see he was tiring and I just had to wait for the opportune moment to strike. Another shot from his right which I blocked with my left hand. I sensed the opportunity and brought my fist driving into his face knocking him sprawling across the floor.

He was inches away from the blazing inferno. He got up to his feet slowly now, he could sense he was losing but it didn't stop him trying. Then everything went into slow motion. A few things happened at once. First he tried another punch which I blocked then sent my foot driving into his chest knocking him off his feet backwards. At that exact moment, the ground beneath him disappeared engulfed by the flames. He was falling back into nothingness. All that was left was a sharp bit of wood protruding from the darkness and he kept falling till he landed on it.

The wood had pierced his body and came out the other side. He had become a human skewer. Blood erupted from his mouth. He managed to lift his head to look at me.

"Son, please help me. I'm still your father" he said weakly tears showing through the blood.

"No. My father died a long time ago" I replied. He took one last look at me then his head fell back and he let out his final breath. Despite it all, I still felt devastated. I felt the tears stream down my face.

I sunk to my knees and sobbed gently, once again mourning the loss of my father as the flames continued to blaze around me.

Chapter 15

The Future

I opened my eyes to a brightly coloured room with halogen lights beaming down on me. The same place I had woken up to every day for the past two weeks. But today was different. Today I finally got to go home. To my new home with Faith.

After the massive fire broke out at the mansion, everybody gathered outside. The fire department were there trying to contain the blaze as best they could but the building collapsed in on itself and extinguished the fire itself. Luckily I wasn't in there when it happened. After the long battle with my father, I didn't think I was getting out of there. I thought about jumping out of the window but I saw what happened to the wolf and didn't think I stood a better chance so I looked in the bedroom. That also didn't look any good but I decided to try under the bed and luckily there was a trap door which I flung open. Inside was a ladder leading down so I jumped down as quick as I could. This eventually led to some stairs which must have taken me away from the mansion. At one point I had a terrible feeling of being buried alive underneath the rubble with no way out but thankfully I came to another ladder, this time leading up and back to the surface.

I ended up a few hundred feet from the wreck that was now the mansion. I realised the trap door must have been there for when my father needed to get out but not be seen. I saw the crowd of people in front of the inferno. I walked back towards the herd of people, hoping to see Ray and Faith. I heard gasps as I made my way through the crowd and it just occurred to me what I must look like. But I didn't care I just wanted to see Faith and relax. I made my way to the front and saw Faith, Ray and Paige. Paige had her face buried into Rays shoulder but I could hear the sobs coming from her. Ray had a look of concern on his face and Faith was just staring intently at the building but it was clear that she had also been crying.

"What a mess" I said weakly. At this they all turned, all three with different looks on their faces. Paige was shocked, Ray a big grin on his face and Faith just looked relieved. Then they all gave me a massive bear hug knocking the breath out of me. I nearly collapsed and would have if it wasn't for them holding me up. All the fighting and near death experiences were catching up with me so they took me straight to the hospital. Now two weeks on, they had finally cleared me to leave. One of the three were usually with me so I wasn't on my own much but I couldn't wait to get out and for the first time and actually start enjoying my life.

"You all ready to leave mate?" Ray asked.

"Like you wouldn't believe" I said with a grin. I still had plenty of battle scars from everything I went through, including my first encounter all that time ago with the first set of wolves. But they were all healing. The one thing I knew that would stay with me and would probably never heal was the thought of my father turning into the man he had. I put the thought to the back of my mind and tried to remember the loving, caring man who raised me on this god forsaken planet. Ray and myself had set off on so many adventures already, it felt like this was the final one which I was sort of pleased about. I'm not sure my body could take much more.

We had been walking for a while, making our way back home when something hit me. I took a look around.

"Its very quiet around isn't it?" I asked Ray.

"Yeah. I hadn't really noticed" he replied. I thought it was strange but I carried on thinking nothing of it. We rounded the last corner back home. It was the most glorious sight. A place I could finally call my own with people I love. Faith and Paige were waiting on the doorstep whispering excitedly.

"Hi ladies" Ray said.

"Hey. Me and Paige were just thinking rather than stay in, we should go out. Now there's nothing to worry about" Faith said.

"I'm kind of tired, I was just hoping for a night in with you three" I said.

"Please" Faith said and I knew I couldn't say no to her. So a couple more minutes later we were going out. They knew not to bring up what happened as it was too painful to think about. I told them once and it was enough for them. Instead they all kept the conversation on the future and what it holds. Something I was very excited about.

We was reaching the main square when I heard a hubbub of noises. We reached the top of a hill and I could see why the place was so quiet. It turned out the whole town was gathered here.

"What's going on?" I asked.

"You'll see" was all Faith replied. Then she grabbed my hand and pulled me into the crowd. I couldn't see anything whilst we fought our way through everybody. Eventually we managed to reach the front which turned out to be a stage with a lectern on top of it. There were microphones on top of the lectern and now I looked around I noticed some speakers scattered around the square. There were also some seats at the back of the stage. I noticed more guards around but I guessed these weren't the same as the ones under my fathers employ. They had slightly different uniforms. Instead of the old US army type of clothing, these were jet black instead. But they were still holding machine guns, hopefully these ones wouldn't be used on me though.

A man walked up on stage. I recognised him at once. His face was all battered and bruised but he looked a million times better than the last time I saw him. It was Marcus the previous leader, the one that Faith and I saw getting tortured. I was able to make out what he looked like now. He was obviously quite old which made the torturing even more abhorrent. His face was covered in wrinkles and battle scars. He had white close, cropped hair with light blue eyes peeking out from behind the bruising and the swelling. He had obviously shaved since being tortured to reveal his face. He was wearing a white cassock with matching pellegrina. He stepped up to the lectern preparing to speak.

"Good evening" his voice boomed over the speakers. His voice didn't match his appearance. To look at him, you would think he was a feeble old man but to hear him, he sounded like a strong confident man.

"My name is Marcus Richman and after years of being tortured by that tyrant." I winced at the mention of him. Faith noticed and gave me a smile to reassure me. I smiled back.

"I am finally free. We are free of his tyranny.

And it's all thanks to some extraordinary people. People who saw what was wrong with this town and went above and beyond to rid this place of its tyranny." I could see why Faith and the others wanted to go out and not stay in. They wanted me to see how grateful people were to us.

"Firstly, I would like to say a huge thank you for not only saving me but saving this whole town and I would like to invite each of them up in turn to say thank you. First up is Paige O'Connor. She showed great resourcefulness in helping to overthrow the tyrant. I would like to invite her up to say thank you and to award her with a special medal for services to the town" Marcus started clapping and everyone else joined in. Rapturous applause filled the air with a couple of whistles thrown in. Paige nudged past me looking shy but she made her way on to the stage and was greeted by Marcus with a handshake and a smile before presenting a medal and placing it around her neck. She stayed on the stage and took a seat at the back of the stage.

"Next I would like to invite up Faith Fear" Marcus continued. Faith shot me a smile before leaving my side and making her way up to the stage.

"She, like me, was kidnapped and tortured but showed great restraint and resilience in the face of adversity. I would like to thank you for your dedication to the cause" he finished just as she reached the stage. She too shook hands and was presented with a medal around her neck. Again applause erupted in the atmosphere and she smiled at the crowd before taking her seat next to Paige.

"Now I would like to invite Ray Miller to the stage". All of a sudden Ray was by my side.

"Make sure you milk it mate. I know I will" Ray said with a wink before making his way to the stage.

"He showed unbelievable courage and excellent fighting skills, even risking his life to help his friends and to help this town so thank you Ray" Marcus said. People again began applauding as he was making his way up to the stage. True to his word Ray began clasping one hand in the other and shaking them victoriously before he got to the top of the stage and began bowing and blowing kisses. The audience applauded louder at this and I couldn't help but laugh. Marcus just looked disapprovingly but nonetheless smiled as he presented the medal to Ray, placing it around his neck. He then took a seat on the other side of Paige.

"And finally, the person who deserves the most thanks and appreciation. This person never gave up even when the odds were stacked against him. He personally took on the tyrant and from what I understand suffered greatly from the battle not just physically but mentally and emotionally. Please join me in saying thank you and give a massive round of applause to Mr Blake Andrews." I looked around nervously and suddenly it felt like everything went silent I could see people clapping but no sound was reaching my ears. I looked at Faith who smiled and suddenly sound flowed back to my ears and I noticed the applause was the loudest yet. It was deafening.

I made my way up to the stage, just praying not to trip and look like a fool in front of everyone but I kept my nerve. Marcus was waiting at the top smiling at me with the medal in his hand. I looked at Ray, Faith and Paige who were all up on their feet smiling and applauding. I shook Marcus hand. He then placed the medal around my neck. I cupped it in my hand and got a better look. It was gold with thank you written across it. I turned it over and saw something engraved on it. It said 'Thank you for your services to this town'. It wasn't much but it meant a lot to me.

"Thank you" I said through the noise of the crowd. They were still applauding.

"One final thing. I would be honoured if you would agree to be my head of security?" He whispered to me. I didn't know what to say. On one hand it was an honour to be asked but on the other, would it be too much pressure for me. It didn't take long for me to make my decision.

"One condition. I have Ray as my deputy" I said gesturing towards him. He was still milking the applause, clasping his hands together and shaking them before blowing kisses towards the crowd.

"I guess" he said with a perplexed look on his face. He then stepped aside and waved me towards the lectern, gesturing for me to say a few words. I stepped in front of it not knowing what to say. The crowd fell silent. I could feel the thousands of eyes staring at me waiting to hear some inspirational speech.

"Umm..." I hesitated.

"First I want to say thank you to Marcus for this medal and thank you to all of you for such warm applause and for accepting me into your community and way of life. Second I want to thank these three sat behind me for following on this perilous journey and for keeping me going. I came to this place full of wonder. Full of awe for what this place was. I had never seen anything like it. All my life, all I've ever known is how to survive in this world. I didn't even know there was other people left till my good friend Ray came into my life. He showed me a new world and I am eternally grateful to him. But my awe for this place quickly turned into horror after I saw how it was ran. How you were treated. I knew I had to do something and thankfully we triumphed over the tyrant." More applause came which I was thankful for. It gave me the chance to compose myself after thinking about how the tyrant was my father. The applause died down again so I continued.

"His reign came to an end but there are still plenty of dangers in this world. Dangers we face everyday. But now as you're new head of security, I will strive to keep my friends safe. To keep this community you have built safe. And to keep this town safe. Tomorrow we get to work at rebuilding but for tonight we celebrate!" I finished with a roar and the crowd erupted giving the biggest cheers yet.

I looked back at Ray, Paige and Faith to see their beaming faces at me joining in the applause. Then I looked at Marcus who also joined in the applause. Then I finally turned to the huge congregation in front of me, all celebrating, smiling, cheering. My thoughts again turned to my father on how he raised me in this world and how much he taught me. I glanced up to the sky sad about what had happened but I decided against remembering the person he had become and focused on who he used to be.

I looked back at everybody celebrating and decided maybe it wasn't such a bad world after all.

Printed in Great Britain
by Amazon